Wemberly Worried

KEVIN HENKES

GREENWILLOW BOOKS

An Imprint of HarperCollins*Publishers*

For Phyllis, who never worries

Wemberly Worried
Copyright © 2000 by Kevin Henkes
All rights reserved. Manufactured in USA.
For information address
HarperCollins Children's Books,
a division of HarperCollins Publishers,
10 East 53rd Street, New York, NY 10022.
www.harpercollinschildrens.com

Watercolor paints and a black pen were
used for the full-color art.
The text type is Usherwood.

Library of Congress Cataloging-in-Publication Data

Henkes, Kevin.
Wemberly worried / by Kevin Henkes.
p. cm.
"Greenwillow Books."
Summary: A mouse named Wemberly,
who worries about everything, finds that
she has a whole list of things to worry
about when she faces the first day of
nursery school.
ISBN 978-0-688-17027-1 (trade bdg.) —
ISBN 978-0-688-17028-8 (lib. bdg.) —
ISBN 978-0-06-185776-8 (pbk.)
[1. Worry—Fiction. 2. First day of school—Fiction.
3. Nursery schools—Fiction. 4. Schools—Fiction.
5. Mice—Fiction.] I. Title.
PZ7.H389 Wg 2000   [E]—dc21   99-34341   CIP

14 15 16 LP 20

First Greenwillow paperback edition, 2010.

Wemberly worried about everything.

Big things,

little things,

and things in between.

Wemberly worried in the morning.

She worried at night.

And she worried throughout the day.

"You worry too much," said her mother.

"When you worry, I worry," said her father.

"Worry, worry, worry," said her grandmother.

"Too much worry."

At home, Wemberly worried

about the tree in the front yard,

WHAT IF IT FALLS ON OUR HOUSE?

and the crack

in the living room wall,

and the noise the radiators made.

At the playground, Wemberly worried about

the chains on the swings,

and the bolts on the slide,

and the bars on the jungle gym.

And always, she worried about her doll, Petal.

"Don't worry," said her mother.

"Don't worry," said her father.

But Wemberly worried.

She worried and worried and worried.

When Wemberly was especially worried, she rubbed Petal's ears.

Wemberly worried that if she didn't stop worrying,

Petal would have no ears left at all.

On her birthday, Wemberly worried

that no one would come to her party.

"See," said her mother, "there was nothing to worry about."

THIS IS THE BEST PRESENT EVER!

I WISH I HAD MY BIRTHDAY TODAY.

But then Wemberly worried that there wouldn't be enough cake.

On Halloween, Wemberly worried

that there would be too many

butterflies in the neighborhood parade.

"See," said her father, "there was nothing to worry about."

But then Wemberly worried because she was the only one.

"You worry too much," said her mother.

"When you worry, I worry," said her father.

"Worry, worry, worry," said her grandmother.

"Too much worry."

Soon, Wemberly had a new worry: school.

Wemberly worried about the start of school

more than anything she had ever worried about before.

By the time the first day arrived, Wemberly had a long list of worries.

What if no one else has spots?

What if no one else wears stripes?

What if no one else
brings a doll?

What if
the teacher
is mean?

What if the room
smells bad?

What if they
make fun
of my name?

What if I can't
find the bathroom?

What if I hate
the snack?

What if
I have
to cry?

"Don't worry," said her mother.

"Don't worry," said her father.

But Wemberly worried.

She worried and worried and worried.

She worried all the way there.

HAVE FUN!

While Wemberly's parents talked to the teacher, Mrs. Peachum,

Wemberly looked around the room.

Then Mrs. Peachum said, "Wemberly, there is someone

I think you should meet."

Her name was Jewel.

She was standing by herself.

She was wearing stripes.

She was holding a doll.

At first, Wemberly and Jewel just peeked at each other.

"This is Petal," said Wemberly.

"This is Nibblet," said Jewel.

Petal waved.

Nibblet waved back.

"Hi," said Petal.

"Hi," said Nibblet.

"I rub her ears," said Wemberly.

"I rub her nose," said Jewel.

Throughout the morning, Wemberly and Jewel

sat side by side and played together whenever they could.

Petal and Nibblet sat side by side, too.

Wemberly worried.

But no more than usual.

And sometimes even less.

Before Wemberly knew it,

it was time to go home.

"Come back tomorrow," called Mrs. Peachum,

as the students walked out the door.

Wemberly turned and smiled and waved.

"I will," she said. "Don't worry."

IDOL GIRLS

What's Your Obsession?

HAYLEY DIMARCO

Revell
Grand Rapids, Michigan

Hungry Planet

© 2007 by Hungry Planet

Published by Revell
a division of Baker Publishing Group
P.O. Box 6287, Grand Rapids, MI 49516-6287
www.revellbooks.com

Printed in the United States of America

Library of Congress Cataloging-in-Publication Data
DiMarco, Hayley.
   Idol girls : what's your obsession? / Hayley DiMarco.
      p. cm.
   Includes bibliographical references.
   ISBN 10: 0-8007-3154-9 (pbk.)
   ISBN 978-0-8007-3154-0 (pbk.)
   1. Teenage girls—Religious life. I. Title.
BV4551.3.D56 2007
248.8′33—dc22   2007025670

Published in association with Yates & Yates, LLP, Literary Agents, Orange, California.

CONTENTS

WHAT'S YOUR OBSESSION?

(aka The Intro)

Do you ever feel like you can't shut your mind off? Do you think and rethink things you've done or said or want to do or say? Is there a certain guy you just can't get your thoughts off of? Or does your mind continually pick on you about your body, your face, your hair, or some other part of you? What takes up most of your thoughts? Are you glad about that or tired of it? What's your obsession?

Is there something that's making you blue? Keeping you up at night or waking you up in the morning? Or answer me this: what's one thing you love so much that you could never live without it? Your favorite pillow? Attention? Clean underwear? What can't you live without?

For me, I love to be comfortable. I love my amazing and oh-so-comfortable bod. I sleep with four pillows all strategically placed around my body. I love comfort. I like a good comfortable car, in a restaurant I like a booth instead of a chair, and I love a comfortable pair of jeans. I'm all about comfort. And I confess right now that it's my obsession at times. I can't get enough comfort. I'll do almost anything to get it. Ugh! Comfort, you evil slave driver of mine! Why must you haunt me so? Okay, sorry for the drama, but really, I feel like a slave to comfort. What are you a slave to? Can you tell me right now, what's your obsession? Let's give it a go and see if we can unearth those little and not-so-little obsessions and see how they make you tick.

Take this handy personal assessment with me, won't you?

WHAT'S YOUR OBSESSION?

What do you love the most? (This may be a long list.)

_____

_____

_____

_____

_____

What would you do to get it or keep it? (Ask yourself this for each thing you listed above.)

_____

_____

_____

_____

_____

Who do you love the most?

_____

_____

What would you do to keep them?

_____

_____

_____

_____

What do you hate the most?

_____

_____

What would you do to get rid of it or avoid it?

_____

_____

_____

_____

What/who do you think about the most?

_____

_____

What are your goals?

_____

_____

_____

_____

What are your biggest fears?

_____

_____

_____

_____

What do you worry about the most?

_____

_____

_____

What do you think you have to have right now?

_____

_____

What "necessities" could you never live without?

_____

_____

_____

_____

What do you do when you need a little peace?

_____

_____

_____

What do you do when you're stressed out and you need
to unwind?

_____

_____

_____

_____

Do you go to something or someone for relief when you are
upset, stressed, or exhausted? If so, who or what?

_____

_____

_____

_____

Does that someone or something give you relief that lasts?

_____

_____

What would you do if you couldn't get that someone
or something?

_____

_____

Who do you trust? Or what do you trust?

_____

_____

_____

Who do you have to please in order to be happy?

_____

_____

Whose opinion is most important to you?

_____

_____

Who are you trying to impress?

_____

_____

What is your biggest obsession?

_____

_____

Did you do it? Did you answer them all? They're tough. But be sure you give them some real thought. If you can't be truthful and thoughtful about this stuff, then it's going to be hard to help you take back your mind and your emotions. So get real.

WHY SO MUCH OBSESSION?

Listen, before we go on, I want you to understand something. Obsession isn't an odd thing. It isn't even an uncommon thing. In fact, it's a part of our natural human affection for worship. It's built into our DNA, this wanting to worship something, wanting to go to it for hope, relief, and help. And whether your love is boys or clothes, worship offers you something: a chance at happiness. Otherwise you wouldn't obsess. You are looking for a payoff. And part of that DNA that we were given was put there to drive us to obsession—but not necessarily the obsessions that you have chosen.

As you might just see in the following pages, some obsessions can make you crazy. They can ruin your life or at least break your heart. What they offer might never come to pass. Obsessions can steal your happiness and peace of mind as quickly as they offer relief. Obsessions can do a number on your life, and that's why reading this book is so important for you. It's about figuring out who you are and what makes you tick.

In fact, *Idol Girls* is a book about you. It's a book that makes you think and think hard about who you are and who you want to become. It would be great if your life could be on autopilot and you could just relax in the passenger seat, feet up on the dash, hands behind your head. But although some people live that way, they aren't the healthy kind of people I hope you want to be. Children of God, that's who we are. People who worship a God who is continually working with us to help make us more like him. If you want to be a faithful follower of your God, if you want to grow closer to him and more holy in your walk, then come with me on the journey of *Idol Girls*. What you find might freak you out, it might make you mad, and it might just change your life both inside and out.

So let me ask you the question I love to ask: if you keep doing what you're doing and living like you're living, you'll keep getting what you've got—is that enough? Or do you want more? More from your life, more from your future, and even more from your past? If you're ready for the journey of a lifetime, then let's go!

If you haven't really, really considered the answers to those questions I asked earlier, then go back and give it some thought. Think about you and your inner workings. What's the truth about you? When you've done that, you'll be ready to go.

OBSESSION—GOOD OR BAD?

An obsession is something that fills your mind and demands you give it attention. That something can be a person, place, or thing. And how you handle it can be good or evil. When it comes to obsessions, people will do whatever it takes to feed the passion, the desire, or the need. Obsession can give you energy or make you weak. It can drive you to success or to insanity.

Vincent van Gogh is a really old, er, really dead painter guy. You've probably seen his work on mouse pads and foofy calendars and such. (Star note: You know you've made it when they put your work on T-shirts and mouse pads!) He's all that in the painting world. His works go for untold millions. He's a household name. But flash back to the days when Vince was alive and kickin' and you'll find the definition of obsession. Okay, maybe you won't find the definition of obsession, but you'll find one obsessed painter.

Vincent was so obsessed with his art that it drove him to insanity. And of course because of that he will be forever remembered as the wacko who cut off his own ear. Talk about drama, huh? Well, Vincent just couldn't bridle his passions. Although he was arguably one of the best painters of his time, he was also the most depressed and crazed. His obsession beat him up and down.

And while we're on the subject of dead painter dudes, let's have a look at the life of Picasso. You've probably seen his stuff all over the place too. His take on the world was, shall we say, unique. Although from his paintings you might assume the man was crazy, he really wasn't as flipped out as our buddy Vince. Pablo, as his friends called him, was so obsessed with his art that he wouldn't let anything get in the way. Labeled a dyslexic in childhood, Pablo had a really hard time making it through school.

He could have let the naysayers—or as some might say, jerks—convince him he was too stupid to succeed, but he didn't. His passion for art and discovering the world around him led him on to greatness in his field. Yep, old, I mean dead, Pablo took his obsession and turned it into a powerful tool for overcoming his obstacles and achieving his goals.

Tons of other guys and gals have done this too. (Did I just say gals? Ugh, I've become my father. Anyway . . .) Tons of people have used their obsession to drive them to achieve, but quite probably just as many if not more have let their obsessions take control of their lives and run them to the ground like a broken-down horse.

Before we go any further, let's have a little look-see at what Webster's has to say about an obsession. For some it is **"a persistent disturbing preoccupation with an often unreasonable idea or feeling,"** while for others it's defined as a "compelling motivation." See, according to Webster and his good old dictionary, an obsession can be used for good or eeeeeeeeeeeevil. (Cue sinister music here.) **Obsession can either make you or break you.** So what's the deal with your obsession? Is it good for you or bad for you? Is it responsible for your misery or your joy? **Figuring out what obsessions are doing to you just might help make your life a better place to be.**

YOUR LIGHT AND DARK
OBSESSIONS

The next part of our journey is into the realm of light and dark. **If you knew that an obsession you were holding was wrecking your life, would you be willing to let go of it?** What about good obsessions? Can they make your life better? The thing I want you to get here is that your life, however great, miserable, or comical it is, can always become better. We all have our bad days and our good days, but for a lot of us there can seem to be more bad days than good. But no matter what the case, a real look at what you obsess about will teach you a lot about yourself and your hope for the future.

Before we delve further into the fixing, let's take another introspective look. I'm getting a lot of this self-analysis out of the way early so your answers won't be colored by what I say later. This beginning stuff is just about you getting real with yourself and starting out with a good understanding of who you are and what you think about. So have a look at these lists and circle the ones that are your real obsessions. Which would you, or the people who know you, say are always on your mind?

My Light Obsessions	My Dark Obsessions
(circle yours)	(circle yours)

My Light Obsessions	My Dark Obsessions
Family	Fear
Friends	Worry
Boy(s)	Self-condemnation
Romance	Sexuality
Being perfect	Superstition
Ministry	Cutting
Happiness	Purging
Comfort	Starving
Food	Indecisiveness
Eating healthy	Complaining
Staying fit	Astrology
Shopping	Gossip
Talking	Revenge
Sleep	Drugs
Patriotism	Unforgiveness
Morality	Shame
Losing weight	Guilt
Being really responsible	Alcohol
Being successful	Gambling
Being in control	
Cleanliness	
Getting married	
Music	
Protecting or worrying over those you love	
Your favorite sports team	
Looking good	
Grades	
Safety	
Being popular	
Your favorite hobby	

SIGNS OF OBSESSION

Next, look at the list below and put an X by any of them that you are dealing with right now.

- ☐ Depression
- ☐ Addiction
- ☐ Social isolation
- ☐ Loneliness
- ☐ Financial loss
- ☐ Weight problems
- ☐ Image problems
- ☐ Anger
- ☐ Bitterness
- ☐ Envy
- ☐ Hatred
- ☐ Never having enough

- ☐ Self-mutilation
- ☐ Hurriedness
- ☐ Desperation
- ☐ Violence
- ☐ Guilt
- ☐ Shame
- ☐ Fear
- ☐ Worry
- ☐ Discomfort
- ☐ Broken heart
- ☐ Anguish
- ☐ Self-hatred

None of this stuff is fun or good for you. **If you are sick of feeling any of these things, then now's your chance to get rid of the bad and bring in the good.** I know it might not seem like it just yet, but I am going somewhere with this. It's important that we take a good self-assessment before we dive into the really meaty stuff. This stuff will really help you once you get it out of the way. So trust me. Go back and do the work if you haven't already, and be honest. This is going to be some trippy stuff, so hang on, here we go!

ISRAELITE IDOL

In the olden days, back when all the fashionable men wore long dresses and sandals around town and donkeys were the main form of transportation, obsessions were all the rage. People obsessed a lot about things like the weather, locusts, fertility, death, the sun, the moon, who would be king, weird stuff like that. They weren't so concerned with music, clothes, or making good grades, but they did have an interesting little episode where the Jewish nation voted on who would be the next *Israelite Idol*. So there's something we have in common: one nation coming together to vote on their next *Idol*. Yep, it was a big event in the olden days too. And talk about obsession! The crowds went crazy. And the winner? The golden calf. Have a look and see what obsession the traveling hordes were into:

Scene from *Israelite Idol*, the Old Testament reality show
(Setting the Scene: The desert. Thousands of Israelites are gathered together. They see that Moses is slow in coming down from the mountain, so they gather around Aaron.)

Israelites: "Come, make us gods who will go before us. As for this fellow Moses who brought us up out of Egypt, we don't know what has happened to him."

Aaron: "Take off the gold earrings that your wives, your sons and your daughters are wearing, and bring them to me."

(Scene: All the people take off their earrings and bring them to Aaron. He takes what they hand him and makes it into an idol cast in the shape of a calf, fashioning it with a tool.)

Israelites: "These are your gods, O Israel, who brought you up out of Egypt."

(Scene: Aaron builds an altar in front of the calf.)

Aaron: "Tomorrow there will be a festival to the LORD."

(Scene: Cut to early morning the next day. Early morning. The people are sacrificing animals and making fellowship offerings. Then they sit down to eat and drink and get up to indulge in revelry.)

Credits: adapted for the screen from Exodus 32:1–6

That really happened. I promise. The Jews, who had been suffering like crazy as slaves making bricks and stuff for the nasty Egyptians, were set free when the sea opened up and they all walked right through it, safe and dry, to the other side. They worshiped God. They loved God. They were the children of God, and Moses and his buddy Aaron had led them out of bondage on their way to a land flowin' with milk and honey. Mmmm. But when Moses took off to go consult with their God, they got a little antsy. See he didn't get back as quickly as they'd hoped, and although they loved God, they felt a bit insecure without the guy who did all their talking for them. They thought maybe God would smite them or something if they didn't have a spiritual leader, so they took matters into their own hands. They went to Aaron, their temporary and oh-so-*not*-Moses leader, and begged him to help. They needed someone to follow, someone to lead them. And a bunch of gold can get you anything, so why not put it all together and make it into a beautiful golden calf? (The Israelite equivalent of William Hung!) It might seem like the stupidest thing ever—make a golden statue to follow when your leader's gone too long—but back then they didn't understand things like we do now. And so for them, that was their best attempt at taking care of things. Their plan was to follow God, it really was; they just didn't go about it in the right way. And boy, you should have seen it when Moses got back—he literally and figuratively pulled a Simon Cowell and melted and ground their idol choice down to smithereens. It was classic. So now every time you see Simon, you're gonna think of Moses, only less holy and in a tight black T-shirt—weird, huh?

So what does this ancient story of golden idols have to do with your obsessions? A lot, really. See, the Israelites were obsessed with having a spiritual leader. So obsessed that they would do anything to

have one—even break one of God's laws (the one about having no idols before God, from Exodus 20:4). Hmm, breaking God's law in order to worship God... seems odd. But it's true. After Moses was gone for forty days, the Israelites couldn't bear it anymore, and their obsession became more important than their obedience. And the result was sickness. **When the Jewish nation obsessed about something other than God, they got sick.** *"And the* Lord *struck the people with a plague because of what they did with the calf Aaron had made"* (Exodus 32:35).

Obsessions have been making people sick since the dawn of time. You tracking with me? Your obsession—or as the Bible calls it, your idol—is making you sick. Don't get me wrong; I'm not saying that if you are sick it's for sure, for sure because of sin. But if you're showing any signs like depression, loneliness, or anger, you could be experiencing spiritual sickness like distance from God, questioning his existence, or wondering if he

even loves you—all stemming from having idols in your life. And it's those obsessions that have gotta go.

"But wait a minute. What's the golden idol have to do with my obsessions?" you ask. "I obsess over stuff that isn't a sin, like my grades, my friends, and my ministry. How is that an idol?" Wow, I'm so glad you interrupted me to ask that. That really helps me make my next transition.

Okay, here's the deal and the reason for this book. Check out Webster's definition of

idolatry:

immoderate [or excessive] attachment or devotion to something

Okay, now look at the definition for

obsession again:

a persistent disturbing preoccupation with an often unreasonable idea or feeling

And *obsess:*

to haunt or excessively preoccupy the mind of

Note the similarities. Yep, **an obsession is an idol.** Plain and simple. Now, don't slam this book down and call me a freak. It's the cold hard truth, and I know you *can* handle the truth. Those obsessions you circled and listed a little while back? Those are idols. Just as much as the golden calf was an idol, so are your obsessions.

It's like this: when you are extremely pre-occupied with something, when it is one of your biggest goals and you do all you can throughout the day to manage it, feed it, or just control it, then you have an excessive devotion to that thing. And **excessive devotion to anything other than God is idolatry.** Okay, so what's the big whoop about idolatry? It seems like such an archaic term anyway. How can it possibly be important in today's day and age?

Let's do a little study and see if we can't clear things up to figure out if idols are a big deal today or not. First let's define idolatry from a biblical perspective. The Ten Commandments starts out with what important topic? Check it out.

> "I am the LORD your God, who brought you out of the land of Egypt, out of the house of slavery. You shall have no other gods before me" (Exodus 20:2–3 NASB).

a. Who is speaking in this verse?

_____

b. Who is he speaking to?

_____

c. What one term is the last part of this verse talking about? _____

The second commandment goes on to clear this idea up. Just in case you couldn't fill in all the blanks (or read upside down), maybe this will help. Here's how commandment number two goes:

"Do not make for yourselves images of anything in heaven or on earth or in the water under the earth. Do not bow down to any idol or worship it, because I am the LORD your God and I tolerate no rivals" (Exodus 20:45 TEV).

a. What does God not tolerate?

_____

b. What is a rival? _____

_____

So **an idol is anything that is a rival to God.** And a rival is anything or anyone who is in competition with or striving to be equal to God. Sounds simple enough. But again you say, "I have no idols, nothing that rivals God or I am attempting to make equal to him." Okay, I hear you, but let's still take a look at what a rival to God might look like in your life.

A rival to God would be in competition with him; therefore it would be something or someone who is fulfilling the same needs or job as God. Someone or something that serves us as well as God or that could meet our needs as well as or better than God, according to our puny little minds. That would mean a rival, or an idol, could be something or someone who might do any of the following:

Make you feel better	Heal you
Give you approval	Complete you
Meet all your needs	Condemn you
Forgive you	Relieve your distress
Give you hope	Tell you what to do to be happy
Save you	
Rescue you	Demand your undying allegiance
Protect you	
Accept you	Occupy all your thoughts

Idolatry is your heart and mind's effort to protect you and to find meaning, purpose, and guidance in something other than God. But believing and trusting God means that you stop looking for ways to save yourself by doing things the world says will save you. Being a follower of the true God means that you don't devote your time and energy to other things and people in an attempt to find relief or hope for yourself. When you put all your energy into something that isn't God but is instead a rival to God, you have become an idolater.

Idolatry is your heart and mind's effort to protect you and to find meaning, purpose, and guidance in something other than God.

SUMMING IT UP

Before we go any further, let's make sure we are all on the same page. So far we've talked about how an obsession can wreck your life, or at least preoccupy it. Then we found out how "idol" and "obsession" can be interchangeable. And then we saw how God gets a little testy when we replace him as the main focus of our lives. See diagram 1 for a quick overview.

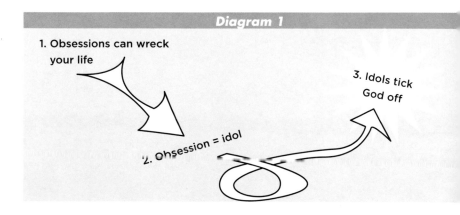

Diagram 1

1. Obsessions can wreck your life

2. Obsession = idol

3. Idols tick God off

WORKING IT OUT

Before we go on, let's work some stuff out. God wants us to understand his Word and to know it in our hearts, i.e., *by* heart. So if you're up for it, let's take this opp to do a little study and memo action. Get out your handy-dandy Bible and do me a favor. Look up the Ten Commandments in Exodus 20. Then write them out here. That would really be supercalifragilisticexpealidocious! (Spell-check please!)

You'd think the whole country would know the Ten Commandments. They're kind of foundational. But no. Very few people know them. In fact, just this year a U.S. congressman who was trying to pass a bill allowing the posting of the Ten Commandments in government buildings was asked by an interviewer if he could name all ten . . . and he only knew four! So wow your friends, have fun at parties, and memorize the Ten Commandments with me!

1. _____

2. _____

3. _____

4. _____

5. _____

6. _____

7. _____

8. _____

9. _____

10. _____

chapter 1

HAPPY GIRLS

I do not like to think of you as needing to have "things" pleasant around you when you have God within you. Surely He is enough to content any soul. If He is not enough here, how will it be in the future life when we have only Him Himself?

Hannah Whitehall Smith

FINDING HAPPY

Here's a stupid question, but as Forrest Gump would say, "stupid is as stupid does," so here goes: **Would you rather be happy or sad?** Joyful or bummed? Unless you're emo, and that's a totally different conversation, then you probably picked happy and joyful because, well, for us sane people it's just more fun and feels better to be happy than sad. Seems obvious, but you never know. If you're sick of being bummed, if you want to get over what ails you, then flop down in your favorite easy chair, scrunch up your favorite pillow, and lean back and enjoy. When you let go of your idols—and don't freak, I'm going to help you with that part too—you will go from dark to light, from sad to happy.

See, here's the sitch. **Idols are happiness stealers.** They come like thieves in the night and steal your joy and delight right out from under you. Oddly enough, they usually come with promises of happiness, relief, or escape, but what they actually do is suck the happy right out of you and leave you feeling empty. See, happiness, or a sense of well-being that we can translate to happiness, is a gift from God. In the Bible they use the word *joy*. I don't use it here because who uses that word anymore? We all say, "I'm happy today," or "I just want to be happy." Not "I'm feeling rather joyous today." Huh? But when we look at the Bible, we're going to be seeing a lot of *joy*. While some would say joy is eternal and happiness is temporary, I call that semantics and find it much more understandable to just think about the older word *joy* as being happy with who you are and what you have. Got it? Okay, so let's have a look and see where true happy comes from. Read the verses and circle with a big heart all the words that mean happy or joyful (♡). And then underline all the references to God, Jesus, or the Holy Spirit, even pronouns like *you* and *he*. I'll do the first one for you.

To the man who pleases him, God gives wisdom, knowledge and happiness.

Ecclesiastes 2:26

May the God of hope fill you with all joy and peace as you trust in him, so that you may overflow with hope by the power of the Holy Spirit.

Romans 15:13

You have made known to me the paths of life; you will fill me with joy in your presence.

Acts 2:28

Do not grieve, for the joy of the Lord is your strength.

Nehemiah 8:10

Though you have not seen him, you love him; and even though you do not see him now, you believe in him and are filled with an inexpressible and glorious joy.

1 Peter 1:8

According to these verses, who gives you happiness (joy)?

_____

What are some of the conditions of receiving this happiness?

_____

How much happiness can he give you? Circle one:
- (a) a little
- (b) some
- (c) all the happy you need

True happiness, unshakable happiness, the really good stuff, comes from God and God alone. If you find that happiness is fleeting or nonexistent, then you might just have an idol to blame. Your obsession, that thing you think will make you happy, is only smoke and mirrors. And what it's doing to your happiness is starving it. When you have an idol, something that rivals God, then your connection to him is short-circuited. A lot of girls complain about not feeling God's presence. They just can't feel him like other people do. In fact, sometimes it makes them question his very existence. The problem is not his existence but your focus. **When your focus is off of God for an extended period of time, your happiness meter drops lower and lower.**

I like playing The Sims. I just love being able to design houses, buy stuff, and have my Sims make money by doing things like sculpture and singing. It's so much fun. If you've ever played The Sims, then you know about your life meters. When you don't pay attention to certain aspects of your Sim's life, their meters empty out. Like if your Sim doesn't go to the bathroom, her bladder meter will drop into the red. And if you don't do something about it, your Sim will wet herself. The same goes for eating and sleeping. You have to take care of all those things in order to grow the life of your Sim. I find it all very challenging and fun.

Think about your happiness on a Sims meter. The more time you spend away from God, the more your true happiness will deplete. Sure, you can do some other things you enjoy, but they don't fill your tanklike time with God. In fact, ultimately they make it so your tank won't fill up at all. And that's why your obsessions can wreak such havoc with your joy. An obsession, or an idol, tears you away from the real source of happiness. It gets in the way and lies to you, promising complete joy if attained. But that's never quite the case.

Believe me, I know that of which I speak. I am the worst of idolaters. I've worshiped some of the most stupid gods ever. And I've paid the price. That's why I did my homework and figured out some of the stuff I'm about to share. I was sick and tired of getting a sugar high from my idols and then crashing a few hours later because they couldn't really deliver what they promised. My idols took away what was rightfully mine: peace, happiness, and a tight relationship with God. And I hate them for it. Well, I guess I actually hate that I went after them. "What an idiot," I tell myself. But enough of this reminiscing. Ugh! If you're sick of feeling sick because of the idols in your life, you are in good company. So let's get to work and kick some golden calf rump roast together. Everything I'm saying to you, I'm saying to me too. Let's do this thing together!

THE IDOL OF HAPPINESS

Before we go any further, since this is a book about idols, I wouldn't be faithful if I didn't warn you that **happiness can become an idol in and of itself if it is your sole goal in drawing nearer to God.** The happiness I have been talking about is a gift from God, but **you should be careful not to worship the happiness rather than God.** It might seem like nitpicking, but here's the deal: a lot of the time we say, "I *just* want to be happy. Being sad is the worst thing in the world." And we become happiness junkies. Anything that doesn't produce happiness is out, and only fun things are in. Bad move! The truth is that happiness isn't the only emotion that is healthy. God makes it perfectly clear by never promising us complete happiness at all times. He tells us we will have trials, we will suffer, we will mourn, and life will be hard, but

My goal is God Himself, not joy nor peace, nor even blessing, but Himself, my God.
Oswald Chambers

that doesn't mean anything is wrong. It merely means we are human. So understand that when I am offering you happiness, I am offering you a chance to shake off the cares of the world and to focus on what matters to God. And that might mean you're suffering or you're struggling, but it will always ultimately mean an unfathomable peace when you are concerned more with knowing God than with merely being happy.

> Do not be anxious about anything, but in everything, by prayer and petition, with thanksgiving, present your requests to God. And the peace of God, which transcends all understanding, will guard your hearts and your minds in Christ Jesus.
>
> Philippians 4:6–7

EMO LOVE

If you're an emo girl who would rather have a good cry about how miserable your life is than get up and make a change, then this all probably seems like insanity to you. Although the whole emo groove (not the type of music but the emotional condition) is a relatively new concept, I know that of which I speak because once upon a time I would have been called emo too. I found great pleasure in going home all alone, getting into a bath, lighting some candles, playing some really sad music, and crying. I would think of all the miserable stuff in my life—and believe me, I found plenty—and then cry about it. It was my favorite pastime. And it would have been my downfall if I hadn't made a change. **When you worship your emotions, explore them, let them rip, and revel in them, you make them little gods.** And little gods demand a lot of attention. Over time they will take complete control of your life, and anything good you ever had will slip away.

If you are emo, let me just say this: I totally understand the choice, but I also know that walking away from it isn't as uncreative as it sounds. My spirit soared only when I decided to ponder not misery but joy. My creative mind grew when I took it off of the subject of my misery and focused it on my hope and future.

God doesn't live in your misery. You won't find him there. You will only find him when you look up and away from your pain. Keeping your eyes on yourself only rots your spirit and your mind. So destroy the idol of misery, and you will start to find God in places you never imagined. Although it may not seem possible now, happiness is actually an option for you, and it is ultimately better than misery.

I'll leave you with this note: being emo is being an idol worshiper. If you wonder what happens to idol worshipers, then keep reading this book. Find out where you're headed and make a decision about changing direction or staying your black course.

Emo Quiz

Take this quiz from my mag *Ask Hayley* to find out if you're an emo queen. If you are an overly depressed or emotional type, you might want to think about making some changes. Don't lie to yourself—God is listening.

1. When I lie in bed, I usually think about:
   a. the bad parts of my day
   b. how to get back at people
   c. all the stuff I'm thankful for
2. When my mind wanders, it's usually stuck on:
   a. thinking of ways to get revenge
   b. worrying about stuff people did to me
   c. the amazing God that I serve
3. Most of the time I feel:
   a. depressed
   b. bored
   c. happy
4. My parents say that I'm:
   a. a whiner
   b. depressed
   c. well balanced
5. When I'm with my friends, we mainly talk about:
   a. how much we hate other girls
   b. how miserable our lives are
   c. how cool our lives are
6. At my school/work:
   a. there is at least one girl who hates me
   b. there are several girls that I can't stand
   c. there are all kinds of people, but I like them all
7. If God is listening in on my thoughts, he is:
   a. not happy with me
   b. not listening anymore 'cuz he's sick of me
   c. proud of me
8. I want to change my thoughts and make them better.
   True   False

Scoring

Add up your points:
1. a = 1, b = 1, c = 3
2. a = 1, b = 2, c = 3
3. a = 1, b = 2, c = 3
4. a = 1, b = 1, c = 3
5. a = 1, b = 1, c = 3
6. a = 2, b = 1, c = 3
7. a = 1, b = 1, c = 3
8. T = 3, F = 1

8-18: Obsessed! Could you be more obsessed with how awful everything is? You don't have to be so down on everything. Remember, you are what you think, so you must be pretty miserable. If you want to feel better, try changing your negative way of thinking to a more positive one. Drop the idol of self and pick up God's Word. It will be a hard change, but you can do it. I believe in you.

19-24: Idol free. At least when it comes to being a downer, you seem to be idol free. Looks like you are focusing on the right things and keeping clean and healthy. Keep up the good work. God is proud of you and so am I.

SHOPPING THERAPY

Ah, shopping. Dreamy! What is it about shopping that is so ex-hilarating? I mean, couldn't you just do it every single day? I could. I've always wanted to find a job where shopping was all I had to do all day. I get goose bumps just thinking about it, and so do millions of other women. **Shopping is like crack for us female types.** Most of us are never too tired to do it and are always certain to feel heavenly after opening that first glass door into fashion heaven. Feeling down? Go shopping. Getting bored? Go shopping. Looking for fun? Go shopping. I mean, it's a cure-all. Shopping therapy, they call it. And boy, can I see why. In his book *Why We Buy: The Science of Shopping*, Paco Underhill says, "We use shopping as therapy, reward, bribery, pastime, as an excuse to get out of the house, as a way to troll for potential loved ones, as entertainment, as a form of education or even worship, as a way to kill time." Yep, yep, and yep. I can relate. Can you? I don't know how many times I've used shopping as my Get Out of Bummersville Free card. And there was a day when I had huge credit card bills to prove it. Oh, yes, I confess shopping is an obsession, or I guess I should say an *idol*, I've managed most of my life.

It's weird how it works, though. 'Cuz I can go buy what are the cutest things ever. The perfect top, fantastic shoes, and all the needed accessories. I wear them once and I feel like a princess. Dreamalicious. Then I wash them and hang them up with all my other stuff, and suddenly I wake up one morning with *nothing to wear*! I mean, what was I thinking? I totally hate that pink top now. Did I ever really like it? And those pointy shoes—could they hurt any more? "Oh, and by the way, your credit card bill came today and it's maxed out." Ugh! It's like coming down off of a sugar high. The fun lasted as long as the trip to the mall, and now I'm sick to my stomach. What's up with that?

My shopping addiction has taught me that idols have a tricky way of sucking out your strength while promising ultimate joy, or at least relief. I dreamed about a pair of boots that I was just sure would bring me complete and utter joy, and a week later I couldn't find them under all my other shoes piled in my closet. Yep, idols offer a lot and never really pay off like promised.

The Bible says to love the Lord your God with all your heart, soul, mind, and strength (see Mark 12:30). Did you catch that? *All* your heart. *All* your soul. *All* your mind. And *all* your strength. When things like shopping, boys, grades, or even homework become your obsession, they become that thing you go to for comfort, hope, or joy. And that takes the *all* out of all your heart, soul, mind, and strength. When you have something in your life that rivals God, then your relationship with him is interfered with. It's like when you drive through a part of town where your XM or your radio gets all staticky and you can't hear your favorite song. It happens to me all the time. XM is satellite radio. It's supposed to be on all the time *and* with no commercials. Both bald-faced lies! But I digress. When I go to Sonic to get a burger and a smoothie, my XM gets all freaky on me. Guess the satellite's not strong enough to beam me through the metal roof. So I back up ever so slowly, just hoping to locate the signal. When I get it, I stop where I am and say, "Ah, Carrie Underwood! I found you." This is what happens when you obsess over something besides God. Suddenly your God-signal gets blurred and you can't see or hear him clearly. When your signal gets all freaky because of an obsession, then you've got to get back where the signal strength is better.

Your happiness and joy comes via that signal, just like your favorite song comes via XM. So if you want more happiness, more joy, more God stuff, then you've got to get out from underneath those obsessions so you can get better reception. Let's unearth those nasty idols that steal what is yours.

Do You Have the Urge to Splurge?

Shopaholic or compulsive buyer: someone who gets a rush from finding that perfect item. Though this "best-dressed" obsession can be as destructive as an eating addiction or gambling, it is most often super hard to spot. The afflicted look cute, put together, and super chic but are most often suffering from financial disarray and emotional upheaval because they never quite have it all. They often change clothes three times or more before deciding what to wear for the day. Their most common statement is "I have nothing to wear!" Sound familiar?

SUMMING IT UP

So here's the recap, just for giggles (and emphasis). If you want to be happy, and I know you do, then you have to look for happy where happy lives: on high. God is the one who gives happiness (aka *joy*) to those who love him and serve him. **If you aren't feeling too good right now, it might just be because of an obsession that's taking all your energy.** See diagram D below.

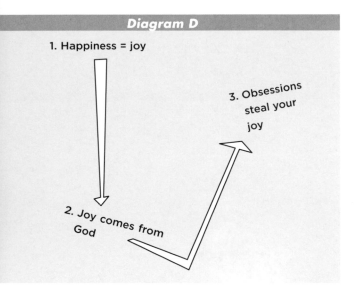

Diagram D

1. Happiness = joy

3. Obsessions steal your joy

2. Joy comes from God

WORKING IT OUT

Let's do a little more Bible study before we go on. Read this verse and then let's dissect it. In the verses below, put a big circle around all the occurrences of *world*. Then put a big heart around all the *love* or *loves*. Put a big cross over every word that means God (i.e., Father, God, him).

> Do not love the world or anything in the world. If anyone loves the world, the love of the Father is not in him. For everything in the world—the cravings of sinful man, the lust of his eyes and the boasting of what he has and does—comes not from the Father but from the world. The world and its desires pass away, but the man who does the will of God lives forever.
>
> 1 John 2:15–17

1. Verse 15: *"Do not love the world or anything in the world."* What does "the world" mean in this text? Does this mean you can't love anything besides God because everything else is "in" the world? That's kind of what it sounds like, doesn't it? But that would be craziness. It doesn't mean you can't love; after all, Jesus commanded us to love (see Matthew 22:37–39). What it means is this: the "world" is anything bad, anything that would cause you to lose track of God or get you so distracted that you'd stop wanting to do what God asks you to do. According to the *Concise Greek-English Dictionary of the New Testament*, the word *world* here really means "men hostile to God, or opposed to His purpose."*

   *Barclay Moon Newman, *Concise Greek-English Dictionary of the New Testament* (Stuttgart, Germany: Deutsche Bibelgesellschaft; United Bible Societies, 1993), 103.

So here's the sitch: if you love things or people more than God, then you don't love God at all. And especially if you love something or someone who hates God, like a nonbeliever, then look out, danger, danger, alert level red! You have walked away from your God. So do a 180 and get back to his side.

2. It's like this: *"For everything in the world—the cravings of sinful man, the lust of his eyes and the boasting of what he has and does—comes not from the Father but from the world"* (verse 16). This just explains it more. If you crave sinful stuff, stuff that God detests, or if you are lusting after something you don't have or someone you want, or if you are bragging about what you have or how good you are, that's all a sure sign that you love the world more than God. That's what all this obsession searching has been about. I'm trying to help you ferret out all the stuff of this world that you love. Why? Because like it says here, all that stuff is going to be gone soon, but when you love God, that lasts forever!

chapter 2

DIGGING UP YOUR HIDDEN IDOLS

Fill in the blank:

"If I only had _____,

then everything would be okay."

WORSHIPING GOD
AND IDOLS?

So what now? You believe in God. Heck, you even love him, and you might not have ever considered yourself an idolater. I mean, those are those freaky guys who worship things like the sun god or wooden idols, not you. You go to church and you love God. **Can a Christian really be an idol worshiper?** The answer is yes. The two aren't mutually exclusive. And you don't have to formally deny God in order to be an idolater. The Old Testament is filled with instances when God's people loved him but also hedged their bets on who would save them by going after other gods, just in case God wasn't quite enough. We already looked at one example, when the Israelites worshiped that golden calf. In Zephaniah—probably not a book you've looked at lately, but you ought to check it out—there is some cool stuff (see Zephaniah 3:17), but I digress . . . anyway, in Zephaniah you can read about actual priests who worshiped God but also another baby god, Molech. Check it out:

> I will stretch out my hand against Judah and against all who live in Jerusalem. I will cut off from this place every remnant of Baal, the names of the pagan and the idolatrous priests—those who bow down on the roofs

to worship the starry host, <u>those who bow down and swear by</u> <u>the Lord and who also swear by Molech.</u>

Zephaniah 1:4–5

See how it says that they "swear by the Lord but also swear by Molech"?

And you've probably heard of Solomon, the guy who wrote the book of Proverbs. Yep, the guy writes a book of the Bible and *still* has idols.

As Solomon grew old, his wives <u>turned his heart after other gods,</u> and his heart was <u>not fully devoted to the Lord his God,</u> as the heart of David his father had been.

1 Kings 11:4

Though Solomon loved God and served him, he also found some other stuff, thanks to his love life (all his wives), that he figured was as good as God. **Lots of people who worship God inadvertently, accidentally, or purposefully turn to other things and people to save them *in addition* to God.** It's like my shopping

You *don't* have to deny God in order to be an idolater.

story earlier. I used to look to shopping to save me from depression instead of looking to God. I didn't hate God or turn away from him to serve the idol of shopping; I just added it in for good measure. So don't think that being a Christian means you don't have any idols. How many times have you said to yourself, **"If I only had _____, then everything would be okay"? If you've ever said or thought that, then even as a believer, you are an idolater.**

Check out more stupid believers following idols:
Micah 3:11; Jeremiah 2:5, 13; Isaiah 2:6–8; Judges 18:30–31; Hayley-in-the-Mall 24/7

YOUR WISH LIST

Wandering the streets, in a world underneath it all. Nothing seems to be, nothing tastes as sweet as what I can't have.

Teddy Geiger

The seaweed is always greener in somebody else's lake.

Sebastian in *The Little Mermaid*

When it comes to digging up your idols, one really easy way is to look at what's on your wish list. What are you counting on to make you happy? The perfect guy? The cutest purse? The best family? What have you seen in other places like in the movies, in your friends' lives, or on TV that you just know in your heart that you have to have? Do you wish for anything enviously or want what someone else has really, really bad? No one is looking over your shoulder, so you can be honest here. Can you think of anything you totally covet? Hmmm?

What's on your wish list right now? (If you need more space, use one of the blank pages at the end of the book.)

What (or who) do you wish for so much that you put all your thoughts toward it (or him)?

What do you just have to have that you don't have?

What one thing, person, or activity could you never live without?

I bet everyone you know has major wish lists of some sort or another. But here's the deal: **when your wish is so powerful that you feel depressed because you don't have it or you stress over never getting it, then you've got problems.** Your whole life can be affected by something you really want but can't get. Believe me, I know. When I was in college I really, really, really wanted someone to love me. I wanted a guy. But try as hard as I could, I just couldn't find one. Then when I got out of college I thought, "Goody, now I'll find a man, and he'll sweep me off my feet, and we'll travel the world together." But alas, he didn't come. It got so bad that it was all I could think about. A lot of girls can say the same thing, especially if it's been a really long time and you are really lonely. Wanting a guy became my obsession. I would cry to God, "Why can't I find a man like all my friends have?" I would watch chick flicks and come home and sit down to a pint of Oreos 'n' Cream just to take the edge off the sting of coming home alone. My wish list, the perfect guy, was making my life miserable because I could never seem to get what I wanted. "Why me?" I moaned with a mouthful of ice cream and another spoonful on the way in.

From a spiritual perspective I can see now why I was getting depressed. When my spirit was yearning for something I didn't have, like true love, it became very dark inside of me. And this kind of spiritual sickness drives a wedge between a believer and their God because it essentially says to him, "*What you've given me isn't enough. I want more!*" The ugly truth is that it's impossible to be thankful and resentful at the same time.

Maybe that's why God warns his children against just such things. **The Bible calls it coveting, and it ain't good!** In fact, imagine my surprise when I read that coveting was—drum

Branjelina and TomKat Love

When I was looking for love, I knew exactly what I wanted—the stuff you see on TV. Or better yet, the stuff you see the stars having and doing. At the time it seemed like everyone had found love but me, and their love seemed so dreamy. Remember Brad and Jen? How cute were they? And Bennifer? Did you see that rock? I was sure they had exactly what I wanted. But truth be told, not everything we dream of is really what we need. If I had found a guy like Brad, I'd be crying in my soup now as I watch him gallivant all over the planet with Angie. And if I'd have taken that humungo rock from Ben, I'd be really depressed watching his "perfect" life with his *new* and ever-so-perky Jennifer. So take a lesson from the "perfect" people: the love you see that you think you want (a la Tom and Katie, Brad and Angie, or Ben and Jen) might not really be as good as you dream it to be. In fact, I bet my editors don't even want me to include these references to Tom and Katie, Brad and Angie, Ben and Jennifer because they know they won't even last until this book makes it into print! I think I've made my point!

Are there things you could do differently to take your dating life with a grain of salt and not be so desperate? Sure, maybe. Check out *Dateable* if you're in high school or *Marriable* if you're 19+, but just don't forget that in general, where you are right now is where you were meant to be. So trust God with your love life and forget about what everyone else has that you want.

roll, please—yes, that coveting was idolatry. Ugh! You mean my wish list could be God's idolatry list? Wowie, zowie. Check it out:

> Put to death therefore what is earthly in you: sexual immorality, impurity, passion, evil desire, and <u>covetousness, which is idolatry.</u>
>
> Colossians 3:5 ESV

God says that when you want something really, really, really bad, you have made that something (or someone) an idol. Does that mean you can't want things? Well, that's a tough question. Let's look at it from this perspective: When you accepted Christ, you also accepted the cross. And that weird expression means that you are to take up your cross and deny yourself. Like the death of Jesus on the cross, your cross should also be that which puts something to death—the old you with all its sinful desires. And that process happens when you deny your urges and your wants and look only toward God and his desires for you. Essentially, when you deny yourself, you walk away from the need to want things other than what God wants for you. So technically I could say that **wanting something, very badly, is not a Christian trait.** Feek. Sounds horrific, doesn't it? I don't mean to be all Mother Teresa on you, but check out some more verses.

> Then he said to them all: "If anyone would come after me, <u>he must deny himself</u> and take up his cross daily and follow me."
>
> Luke 9:23

> Then he called the crowd to him along with his disciples and said: "If anyone would come after me, <u>he must deny himself</u> and take up his cross and follow me."
>
> Mark 8:34

So whether you eat or drink or whatever you do, <u>do it all for the glory of God.</u>

1 Corinthians 10:31

What do you think it means to "deny yourself"?

_____

_____

_____

In what ways do you deny yourself?

_____

_____

_____

In what ways do you refuse to deny yourself?

_____

_____

_____

What does it mean to do everything for the glory of God?

_____

_____

_____

Some people, especially those who are afraid of or hate God, would say that this stuff sounds like a mean, power-hungry God wanting people to be unhappy, poor, and miserable in order to make him happy. "Why would a good God ask you to deny yourself?" they ask. And I can understand why they might think that way. To the world, denying yourself sounds like crazy talk. After all, we're supposed to _be all we can be, take the world by the horns,_ and _have it our way._ A person who doesn't have a God who loves them *has* to take care of themselves and do all they can to get what they want. After all, if they deny themselves, who will take care of them? But a person who has a God who has adopted them and made them his child has something very, very special. This kind of person knows that no matter what, if God said it, then it's the best. Even when God says something so completely nutso as to deny yourself.

When you research God's Word and spend time understanding who he is and what he wants for us, you start to see the beauty in denying yourself. Amazing things come from such a position of selflessness. Because we as believers know that our natural tendency is to be sinful, we understand that "self" can often lead us into trouble.

THE BEAUTY OF DENYING YOURSELF

The look of Jesus will mean a heart broken forever from allegiance to any other person or thing.

Oswald Chambers

Denying yourself isn't just a spiritual exercise that yields only a kind of distant holiness and rugged self-discipline; it is an essential part of the faith of a believer and pays off big when it comes to your ultimate happiness. If you really look, I think you will find that most of your emotional misery comes from wanting something you don't have. Although at first giving up wanting people to love you and stuff to surround you can seem like a really hard thing to do, the truth is that **once you give up wanting what you don't have, you give up being miserable.** Think about it: you're miserable because you don't have a boyfriend. You really want to be loved, but you can't find a guy who likes you. Or you're miserable because some girl is telling lies about you. You want people to like you for who you are, but she's spreading all kinds of rumors about you. **What's really making you miserable is not the other people or things around you but your thoughts about those people and things.** When you covet, you're miserable. When you want what you don't have, you're miserable. Miserable, miserable, miserable.

So what's the solution? *Make* people like you? Steal enough money to buy those shoes you are dying to have? Sounds pretty stupid, don'tcha think? Okay, so you wouldn't go to those lengths, but what else could you do? You're powerless. Or at least that's how you feel. But the truth is, you are powerful. **You have the power to feel better just by changing how you think.** When you "deny yourself" and stop wanting what you don't have, you don't become a weak, self-hating person; you become a free person. The freedom that comes from not "needing" what you don't have is exhilarating. See, when Jesus tells you to deny yourself and take up your cross, he knows what he's talking about. Denying yourself makes life more livable. And ultimately more holy.

This holiness comes because your cross, your burdens and trials, draws you closer to God. The more tough something is to do, the more you need him. And the first place to look when you need him is his Word. If you want more of God, if you want to hear him, feel him, and touch him, then you have to regard his Word as your power. When you read his Word, you'll find one

Most of your emotional misery comes from wanting something you don't have. Once you give up wanting what you don't have, you give up being miserable. Trippy, huh?

strong message, and that is that in order to become more holy and closer to God, you have to give up the right to care what happens to you. Denying yourself and taking up your cross means that no misunderstanding, misinterpretation, slam, insult, or attack against you disturbs you anymore. You remain content because you trust God and believe that nothing happens to you unless he allows it for your benefit. I know this might sound impossible, but God knows it isn't. And that's why he's commanded it.

> But how is it to your credit if you receive a beating for doing wrong and endure it? But if you suffer for doing good and you endure it, this is commendable before God. To this you were called, because Christ suffered for you, leaving you an example, that you should follow in his steps. **"He committed no sin, and no deceit was found in his mouth." When they hurled their insults at him, he did not retaliate; when he suffered, he made no threats. Instead, he entrusted himself to him who judges justly.** He himself bore our sins in his body on the tree, so that we might die to sins and live for righteousness; by his wounds you have been healed. For you were like sheep going astray, but now you have returned to the Shepherd and Overseer of your souls.
>
> 1 Peter 2:20–25

Remember that nothing God commands you to do is impossible. He gives you the power to do it all. According to God's Word, we are to walk like Christ, in his steps—"you should follow in his steps" (verse 21)—and when you do that, you leave no room for self.

The best way for you to take a step toward dying to self is to ferret out all your idols and to smash them. Someone unconcerned with self has no need for idols. So let's keep on with the journey toward digging up your idols and getting rid of them.

When Denying Yourself Is Wrong

Dying to self and denying yourself are godly actions, but they too can become idols. Beware that you don't attempt to die to self in order to punish yourself or others. Dying to self is only holy when it's done in service to God—in other words, when you do it that you might kill your idols or stop a sin in your life. So beware of using the act of dying to self as a selfish act (more on this later). *"These are matters which have, to be sure, the appearance of wisdom in self-made religion and self-abasement and severe treatment of the body, but are of no value against fleshly indulgence"* (Colossians 2:23 NASB).

If you cannot die to self, you can never accomplish what your heart desires.

Sanctification has
a double aspect.
Its positive side
is vivification,
the growing and
maturing of the new
man; its negative
side is mortification,
the weakening and
killing of the old
man.

J. I. Packer

NEEDS VS. WANTS

Before we go any further, I want you to understand that God knows your heart. He knows your thoughts and your motives, and he is not one to condemn you for doing something you didn't know was wrong. Thank God! But now that we are starting to shine the light on the idols in your life, you have to make a change. You must take a closer look at those things that are rivals to God, those obsessions that might just be idols in disguise, because now you know the truth. And **if you don't take a real inventory of your heart, you will continue to worship the creation rather than the Creator.** I know that you are reading this book because you seek to be more holy. You desire to serve God and to love him, and therefore I know that this study of the idols in your life, though it may be hard to swallow, will still tug at your heart and compel you to do something. So before we lose the fire, let's walk forward and check out the idols we have been believing were healthy obsessions or just good comfort in a crazy, mixed-up world.

I'm sure you know the difference between needs and wants. And you probably know where I'm going with this section. But let's just pretend you don't and instead take another little inventory of things you need and things you want. In the space below, make your lists, and then we'll talk about them:

Needs	Wants

According to Webster's dictionary, a **need** is "a physiological or psychological requirement for the well-being of an organism" and to **want** is "to have a strong desire for" something.

Okay, so we all know that a "need" is something you have to have to live—essentials like food, water, and shelter. But sometimes the line between "needs" and "wants" blurs a little. Like when I say I really *need* an alarm system. I want to be safe at night and I don't want anyone to break into my house, so I *need* an alarm. Listen, unless I can eat or drink the alarm, then a need it is not. In fact, I live in one of the safest neighborhoods in the universe now (after living in a high-crime area for a long time). An alarm's really more of a want, wouldn't you say? But I'm all about my "needs." Believe me, my "needs" list is humungoid. Guess I go a little overboard in the "I gotta have it!" department.

Can you relate? Do you have any "needs" that on second glance might really just be wants? Do you see any things listed on your needs list that aren't essential to life? If so, cross them out and move them over to wants. And just in case you're saying, "Well, those new Sketchers *are* essential," let's have a closer look, just to get back to basics. Here are the main categories for needs:

> basic shelter
> basic food
> basic clothing

Do all your needs fit into these "basic" categories? If not, then move-y, move-y, move-y, Little Miss Groovy.

Just to top off the explanation, a *want* is a thing, an activity, or a service that might make your life better but isn't absolutely essential to life. And here are some examples that you might relate to:

> eating out
> car
> computer
> cell phone
> music
> amazing clothes
> makeup
> vacation
> boys
> friends
> TV

So, like I said before, if any of these are in your "needs" column, move-y, move-y, Little Miss Groovy!

Okay, now, in the space below list all those things that moved from the needs pile over to the wants pile.

Okay, so **the best place to start looking for hidden idols in your life is in this pile o' wants right here.** Yep, the minute you wrote down a "want" in the "needs" column, you potentially unearthed a hidden idol. If you can look at this list and say to yourself, "Oh, I get it. I totally wasn't thinking. Of course that was a 'want' and not a 'need.' My bad!" well, then maybe that isn't an idol for you. But let's keep digging just to make sure we've really gotten to the truth of the matter.

There's always the potential with this list that you were subconsciously or even consciously telling yourself that you had to have this something or someone or your life would be miserable and therefore you "needed" it in order to live. And having a strong desire for something isn't bad in and of itself, but the fact of the matter is that these "needs" can become a compelling force in

your life. And **when they compel you to sin when you can't get what you want, they have become idols.** See, idols don't always start out as evil things like demons, addictions, and superstitions; they can be good things that you just want too much. For example, when my need for safety or comfort propels my life and controls it, then the pursuit of it has become a religious act for me, a god in safety's clothing that I worship in order to be protected from the evil in the world. I become more obsessed with my need for security than my trust in God.

So if you are feeling sorry for yourself because you don't have all that you think you "need" (Boy, did I need to hear that right now! Sorry, just thinking out loud.), or if you are thinking about getting revenge on someone because they haven't treated you how you think they should have, you are choosing to sin because you haven't gotten what you wanted or you think you need. It's a nasty little secret that the world tries to keep from us. The perfect dream fills our heads with hopes of pure perfection. The perfect guy, the perfect pair of pants, and shoes that never hurt your feet; the perfect family, straight A's, and a perfect body—they all become goals worthy of your pursuit. And though none of these things are evil in and of themselves, they can easily become so if you are obsessed with them or hating life because you don't have them. That resentment created by not having what you want or think you need leads to the covetousness we talked about earlier, and that, plain and simple, is sin.

So I'd say that for all of us, **it's time to take a long, hard look at when we say the words "I need . . ."** We've got to check ourselves before we wreck ourselves. What are you afraid to say no to? What idol is knocking at your door begging to be let in or sleeping under your covers right now as we speak? Don't let the world lie to you and convince you that you have needs! The only needs you really have are for food, air, water, and shelter. If you have those things, all others are gravy, baby.

The way I see it, idols can come in two distinct forms, light and dark. Light idols are those things that are good when kept in perspective. Things like friends, family, and health. Things that in and of themselves aren't idolatrous. But when these good things become your obsession, look out, idol alert.

WHEN LIGHT IDOLS GO BAD

I have a friend who is really into taking good care of her body. She eats really healthy. Lots of veggies and fruits. No fat and no junk food. Sounds good, right? Well, you would think so, but being "healthy" has become her idol. She won't touch anything "unhealthy," as if it would be sacrilegious. Because for her, eating healthy food has become her own religion. When good things control what you do, they become your god. And refusing at all costs to touch "unhealthy" food to your lips makes healthy food, and the pursuit of it, your obsession or idol.

By the way, this obsession with food often degrades into eating disorders. Why? Because once this little god has control of you, his job is to destroy you. And the easiest way for him to do that is through food, or the lack thereof. And the ironic thing is that most girls who have eating disorders feel like the obsession puts *them* in control, but in reality, it's exactly the opposite. The eating disorder becomes the golden calf, a little god with a little g. So even good things like eating healthy and being safe can become your idols if you run your life around them—or rather they run your life.

Remember the list of light obsessions you circled a while back on page 19? If you hate living in the past and don't want to flip back (or are just a lazybones) here's the list again. Have a look at the list and remind yourself which ones you circled. You might even need to circle some more!

Light Idols

Family	Being really
Friends	responsible
Boy(s)	Being successful
Romance	Being in control
Being perfect	Cleanliness
Ministry	Getting married
Happiness	Music
Comfort	Protecting or worry-
Food	ing over those
Eating healthy	you love
Staying fit	Your favorite sports
Shopping	team
Talking	Looking good
Sleep	Grades
Patriotism	Safety
Morality	Being popular
Losing weight	Your favorite hobby

Does it shock you how many you circled as your obsessions? Now that you know that these obsessions are your idols, do you see them in a different light? Look at a couple of them and think about how they have propelled your life. How have you acted based on these obsessions? **What things have you avoided because of them or done because of them?** How do they make you feel when you don't get them? Or when you do? What things have you forsaken to get them? Have you turned your back on God because of them? Or distanced yourself from him? Hurt someone to get them? Or been made miserable in pursuit of them? Has the search for them made you exhausted? Think about your life and each of these light idols. How have they controlled you?

If you didn't circle any at all the first time you read them, do you see now that maybe you should have? If any of these things control your actions or help you make decisions based

on getting them, then you should have circled them.

One question that helped me to find my many, many light idols was, **"If I'm _____, then I'm not happy."** You could fill in all kinds of things: "If I'm uncomfortable, then I'm not happy." "If I'm cold, then I'm not happy." "If I'm unpopular, then I'm not happy." It's a freaky thing to realize, but when you can make a statement like that, you've just discovered an idol. That's because nothing on earth should control your happiness. As the apostle Paul said, "I have learned the secret of being content in *any and every situation*, whether well fed or hungry, whether living in plenty or in want. I can do everything through him who gives me strength" (Philippians 4:12–13, emphasis added). Think about Paul's life. Imagine if he had said, "I just can't be happy unless I'm comfortable." He couldn't have written the things he wrote in the Bible, because his life was anything but comfortable. His bed was a cold dirt floor in a prison, and he was separated from all his family and friends. He faced a shipwreck, stoning, beatings, so many terrible things in his life, yet he didn't complain or demand to be delivered from it all in order to be happy and productive. It's just not a biblical statement to say, "If I'm _____, then I'm not happy." And if you can make that statement, then you have found an idol.

What You Want Can Kill You

One of the biggest ironies of obsession is how easily you can be hurt by the very thing you desire. It's like the mouse being caught in a trap by the cheese. Or the fish being caught by the worm on the hook. But hey, at least animals have a reason for risking death—the stuff looks like sustenance. Humans can't say the same thing. The idols that take over our lives are most often pure indulgence. No one has to buy a pair of shoes or take another drink. Finding when your desires have become obsessions is the challenge ahead of you, and it will be one of the most difficult you'll ever face. But it's the only way to be idol free.

Cleanliness Next to Godliness?

I know many people of the female persuasion who are obsessed with cleaning. They say things like, "If everything isn't spotless, I'm not happy." I mean, they have to have everything in its place. And that seems like a really good thing, right? Cleanliness is next to godliness, they say. But they lie. That isn't true. And when getting things clean becomes more important than being with the ones you love, or caring for people who need you, or serving God, well, then cleaning has become your idol. A woman named Martha had the same problem back in Jesus's day. She was so obsessed with making everyone a great meal, with "serving" them, that she didn't spend any time with the very one she wanted to serve, Jesus. And for that reason, cooking and serving became Martha's idol. (Check it out in Luke 10:38–42.)

MANAGING YOUR LIGHT IDOLS

Unlike other kinds of idols, **light idols cannot always be avoided.** If your idol is drugs, then it's a no-brainer; you have to stay away from them, avoiding them at all costs. But if your idol is ministry or cleanliness, it can't just be avoided in order to be controlled. Light idols have to be managed instead of completely avoided. Since light idols are often needs or honorable wants that have gotten out of control, they have to be taken charge of. For me, clothes can easily be an idol. For most of my life I've overspent, charged, and gone into debt. I've often made my bad day better by shopping and told people that shopping was "the best therapy for depression." So I know all about loving those light idols.

But since clothing is a necessity, I can't just stop shopping cold turkey. Choose to walk around naked every day in order to be holy and idol free? Nope, not gonna do it. Wouldn't want to scare ya! So if I have to shop and I have to buy clothes, how do I manage my fashionistic idol?

The thing that worked for me when it came to "clothes whoring" was a budget. I now have a cash clothing budget each month. It's all I can spend for all things clothing. And ba-da-bing, ba-da-boom—because of that budget I have magically taken control of the shopping and stopped its oh-so-glamorous hold on me. Though I still crave buying almost everything cute that I see, I don't. Because when the cash is gone, the cash is gone, and I can't charge anything anymore. Believe me, if I could, I'd be right back to worship at the feet of the almighty shopping therapy! But thanks to the cash budget and ditching the credit cards, I can be idol free.

Of course, if your idol isn't one that you pay for, then you'll have to come up with another kind of budget. You can budget your time. Like if exercise is an idol to you, then it's time to budget your workout time. Talk to an expert. Find out how much exercise you need just to be healthy or to maintain your performance level for your sport, and then do no more. You have to learn to keep your light idol in check in order to keep it from controlling you and becoming your new god.

Light idols can be tough because it's like being an alcoholic who works as a bartender. You are always around it, but you can't let yourself get hooked on it again. Enlisting the help of a friend, counselor, or pastor is another good way to get charge of your life again. Talk to people who love you about your obsessions and your worship of your light idol, and then work on a plan to manage your time with that thing. If a friend or friends have become your idol—you organize your entire life around them, you obsess about what they are doing with or without you—then you have to get some help managing that obsession. Talk to your parents about helping you not talk on the phone so much and not spend so much time with them. Work out a schedule where you spend more time with your family, reading the Bible, in prayer, studying, and so on. Just cut back on the amount of time and energy your heart and mind spend on friends.

The next thing you have to do in order to manage light idols is to manage your thoughts about those idols. Just like any other idol, you have to call it out and admit your obsession. Then you have to confess it to God and repent from it. I'm gonna talk more about this in chapter 4, "Idol Free." So let's move on to some other stuff before we get back to the managing.

DEALING WITH DARK IDOLS

Good things can easily become evil in the sight of God when they are rivals for his love—when they compete with his commands, with his Word, and for your obedience. But what about those dark things we listed a while back? Do you remember those? They seemed a bit more obviously bad, and so you might not have checked many, if any at all. But if you did, flip back to page 19 and have a look at those too. Here is the list again to remind you:

Dark Idols

Fear

Worry

Self-condemnation

Sexuality

Superstition

Cutting

Purging

Starving

Indecisiveness

Complaining

Astrology

Gossip

Revenge

Drugs

Unforgiveness

Shame

Guilt

Alcohol

Gambling

These things might seem obviously bad for you and maybe even obviously evil, but have you ever thought about them as idols? Probably not. Sure, shame isn't a great feeling, nor is guilt. But did you realize they can be worse than unhealthy? They can be idolatrous. If any of these things are your obsession, you're dealing with a dark idol. **When you look for comfort in something that can never deliver it, you give darkness a foothold.** These dark idols can be tools of Satan to draw you closer to him and farther from God. When they are things that are most definitely not of God, beware your attachment to them and therefore to darkness. In the words of the apostle John, *"God is light; in him there is no darkness at all. If we claim to have fellowship with him yet walk in the darkness, we lie and do not live by the truth. But if we walk in the light, as he is in the light, we have fellowship with one another, and the blood of Jesus, his Son, purifies us from all sin"* (1 John 1:5–7). **Dark idols separate us from the Father and cause us to live a lie.** Notice that we have fellowship with God only when we walk in the light. But read on. If you have a dark idol, don't despair; all is not lost. We all mess up and we are all guilty. The apostle goes on to say in verses 8–10, *"If we claim to be without sin, we deceive ourselves and the truth is not in us. If we confess our sins, he is faithful and just and will forgive us our sins and purify us from all unrighteousness. If we claim we have not sinned, we make him out to be a liar and his word has no place in our lives."* What this tells us is that there is hope for the followers of dark idols just as there is hope for light idol worshipers. And that **hope is in a simple thing called confession.** When you confess, God is faithful to his Word, and he will not only forgive you but also purify the stuff right out of you. Yep! Read that verse again to get it.

Each one of the dark idols listed on page 19 constitutes sin. And sin has to stop. So it's time to dig into God's Word and bathe

yourself in truth so that when you confess, you can repent and stop that idolatry forever.

I know it isn't easy. You've tried other things before. You know it's wrong, but it's just too powerful. Bah humbug! That's a pile of poop. *"No temptation has seized you except what is common to man. And God is faithful; he will not let you be tempted beyond what you can bear. But when you are tempted, he will also provide a way out so that you can stand up under it. Therefore, my dear friends, flee idolatry"* (1 Corinthians 10:13–14). **It's a lie of the enemy that tells you it's just too hard to stop.** Don't believe it anymore. You can't! Idolatry, or choosing your love of sin over God, is like playing with fire. And I promise you one day you will get burned. The longer you hang on to your dark idol, the more dangerous and deadly it gets. Its "soul" goal is to rip you from the hands of the Father. Don't think that just because you believe in him you are safe even though you have no intention of giving up your idol because it's just not true.

God's Word is filled with what *is* true, however, and that is that if you keep this up in spite of knowing it to be idolatry, you risk missing out on eternal life with the Father. Need proof? Or do your idols need it? Give them this:

Outside [of heaven] are the dogs and the sorcerers and the immoral persons and the murderers and the idolaters, and everyone who loves and practices lying.

Revelation 22:15 NASB

For you may be sure of this, that everyone who is sexually immoral or impure, or who is covetous (that is, an idolater), has no inheritance in the kingdom of Christ and God.

Ephesians 5:5 ESV

Therefore do not pronounce judgment before the time, before the Lord comes, who will <u>bring to light the things now hidden in darkness and will disclose the purposes of the heart.</u> Then each one will receive his commendation from God.

1 Corinthians 4:5 ESV

In these verses God warns habitual practicers of sin—and idolaters, those who worship something other than him—that even though they claim to love God, if they have turned away from him, they should not believe they will inherit the kingdom of God. Idols compel you to continually sin to get them—or because you don't have them—so these verses apply to you too if you're not dealing with your idols. (Note: These verses don't apply to occasional sin—sin that you slipped into and then repented of, like when King David slept with Bathsheba but saw the sin in it and repented.) At one point you didn't understand that those obsessions in your life interfered with your worship of God. But now that you are aware of your idols, you must forsake them, or turn away from them, in order to save yourself from forsaking your God.

Remember, God knows the desires of your heart, he knows your motives, and he will know if you have chosen to hate your idols because you've seen them for what they really are. I don't expect that you will conquer all of them in one fell swoop; I know I haven't. And that's okay. It's the condition of your heart that really matters. In the words of the psalmist, "*The sacrifices of God are a broken spirit; a broken and contrite heart, O God, you will not despise*" (Psalm 51:17 ESV). **When your heart breaks over your idolatry, when you crave repentance and want nothing more than to stop the sin, God is pleased.** So take one step at a time. First admit the sin. Call it what it is. Stop lying to yourself and believing that these obsessions are a healthy part of your life. Then repent and turn away from all your idols. You might slip back into the habits you've had for so long, but over time, with constant readjusting and by seeking God, you will overcome your idols.

SUMMING IT UP

You may have been worshiping a lot of things without even knowing it. Your wish list and your needs list can help point you in the direction of your idols. If you want to be faithful and turn from idols, then you must deny yourself and take up the cross. Give up the right to feel sorry for yourself, to covet what isn't yours, and to demand that things be a certain way, and you can start to be free from idols. See diagram H for a quick overview:

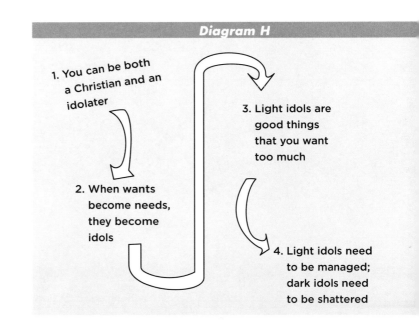

Diagram H

1. You can be both a Christian and an idolater

2. When wants become needs, they become idols

3. Light idols are good things that you want too much

4. Light idols need to be managed; dark idols need to be shattered

Knowing God

without knowing our own wretchedness makes for pride. Knowing **our own wretchedness** without knowing God makes for despair. Knowing Jesus Christ strikes the balance because he shows us both God and our own wretchedness.

Blaise Pascal

When you get too deeply entrenched (involved) in a certain sin, an idol is created. And once an idol is carved, Satan has gained a foothold in your life and can begin his takeover.

Chuck Swindoll

WORKING IT OUT

Sometimes other people know your idols better than you do. You can be too close sometimes to even recognize them. Feeling brave? And in need of humbling? Ask your family and friends what they think you are most obsessed about. You might be surprised what they say. But don't get mad at them. Just take note of the things that others see as your obsession and then talk to God about it. Find out if it's a bad thing or a good thing. Like if you're obsessed with worshiping God, then it's probably not a big deal, but if you're obsessed with getting Mr. Perfect to notice you, then "Idol in the house!" So ask at least two people today what they see as your obsessions. If they ask why, you can explain *Idol Girls* to them. Who knows, they might want to get a copy themselves and get idol free along beside you!

When you find out what others are seeing that you don't, make your list below. We'll work on it as we go through the book.

chapter 3

MY FAVORITE
IDOLS

The human heart is a factory of idols. . . . Every one of us is, from his mother's womb, expert in inventing idols.

John Calvin

I've been talking a lot about idols—shocking for a book called *Idol Girls*, I know! Anyway, you've taken all the tests, asked yourself all the questions, and found a few things you never realized you were obsessed about. But you still might not be sure if everything you've written down is really an idol or just something you really, really like. Fair enough. I know it can be hard to learn the sport of idol spotting. And so I'm here to help. (Cue superhero music!) This chapter is going to get into the nitty-gritty to help you spot the idol in yourself. If any of these things are on your wish list or your needs list— take the time to read about them. If they don't apply to you, skip 'em. Move on if you want, but read what you can and what you like. You never know when you might find a dark spot that needs some light shined on it.

RELATIONSHIP IDOLS

ROMANCE

On a scale of 1 to 10, how important is romance to you? What's your favorite genre of movie? Romantic comedy? Would you give anything to find Mr. Perfect and to ride off into the sunset on a beautiful white horse? What was your favorite fairy tale growing up? Was it romantic?

Romance is dreamy. I adore it. There's just something about it that makes me warm all over and as happy as happy can be. I would love to have a life filled with nothing but dreamy, romantic moments. Romance is not a sin, but wanting it (or *needing* it) could be. If you are depressed because you don't have any romance in your life or you get mad when your boyfriend is clueless about it, then you're addicted to romance. **If you fantasize about romantic love or you covet someone else's dreamy relationship, either fictional or real, then you are addicted to romance.** Romance is an idol that you might not have thought of, but I want you to give it some real, heartfelt consideration. Are you addicted to romance?

How do you feel after going to a good romantic comedy? A little depressed because you aren't going home to Matthew McConaughey or Ben Affleck? Or hot and bothered and in need of a cold shower because of the excitement of an amazing romance? If romance causes you to covet what you don't have, to dream of it, to cry over it, or to complain about it, then romance is an idol for you, and it's time to let that idol go.

Look at your life and see what kinds of things make you wish you had love and romance. What kind of stuff feeds the flame? If romance is your idol, then **these are the things you should avoid: romance novels, chick flicks, romantic music, daydreaming about romance, star mags, and anything else that gets your**

romantic muscle working. (There's more help for the romantically addicted on pages 102–3.)

MEAN GIRLS

Do you have problems with a Mean Girl? If you have serious girl troubles and all you can think about is getting rid of her, then you might just have an idol in your midst. Girls shouldn't be mean. They shouldn't do to you those cruel things they are doing. But the second that you decide to get back at them or start obsessing over what they are doing or saying about you . . . you see where I'm going with this? **You have created an idol out of your archenemy.** Silly thought, isn't it? I mean, you hate her, so why would *she* be your idol? Simple: because she controls your thoughts, or rather the thought of her controls you. And if those thoughts involve revenge or hatred, then she is helping you to sin, and that's what an idol does. If you have serious Mean Girl problems, check out my book *Mean Girls: Facing Your Beauty Turned Beast.* It's a big and very hard topic to handle, and I can't do it all here. But if you have an obsession, no matter if it's a Mean Girl or a hot guy, then it's gotta stop. So get some help and get her out of your mind.

BOYS

I'll admit, boys are an amazing part of life. To have one around is great fun, but if you're pining for a guy you can't quite land, or if *all* you think about is the guy you've got, then something is wrong. **Boys can easily become our idols when we start to think they are the only way to be happy.** Girls who have boys as idols say things like this: *"I just can't be happy unless I'm dating someone." "Of course I'm miserable—I don't have a boyfriend." "I'm so depressed because the guy I like is dating someone else." "Why hasn't he called?"* Are you boy crazy? Then you're obsessed.

Do You Have a Mean Girl Problem?

Answer the following to find out.

1. When you walk down the hall most of the time, you are:
   a. alone
   b. with your gang
   c. with your best bud
2. Sometimes you:
   a. get laughed at by other girls
   b. make fun of the not-so-popular girl's clothes
   c. hang with your friends and have so much fun you forget it's time to go
3. You know how it feels to:
   a. be gossiped about
   b. make someone look bad so you look good
   c. care for a friend who is hurt
4. You spend hours:
   a. worrying about how not to be seen by other girls
   b. thinking about how to get even with someone
   c. helping your friends through tough times
5. When you go to school you are:
   a. afraid to go to the bathroom alone
   b. lovin' life
   c. counseling your friends about all their problems
6. Your parents:
   a. would say you worry a lot about going to school
   b. know that you are happiest when you are with your friends
   c. taught you how to care for others
7. At least once a week:
   a. another girl laughs at you or picks on you
   b. you talk about another girl in a way that puts her down
   c. you try to make your friend feel really good about herself

8. You have cried at school:
   a. many times
   b. only occasionally when a guy is a jerk
   c. not really at all, because you save that for your bedroom

Now add up your scores: a = 3; b = 2; c = 1

18–24: MG obsession. You probably have to deal with at least one girl who is out to get you. But don't let her turn you into a Mean Girl yourself. Revenge makes you a real Mean Girl, and even thinking about it makes you obsessed. So be obedient to God and avoid sinning just because she compels you.

11–17: MG. Did you ever think that you might be the Mean Girl of someone's nightmares? This quiz isn't a perfect diagnosis, but if you're actively "getting her back" or "defending yourself," then she has become your obsession.

8–10: No MG for you. You probably are the one helping the victims of MGs. You see the pain they cause but have mostly stayed free from their attacks. You'll be in a great place if you can learn more about them so you can help more than you do right now. You are the key to solving the troubles between these girls. Never stop being faithful.

Boys aren't the answer to all your woes. They aren't the one thing you need in order to be happy. They aren't even essential to your life. I admit, at one point in my life, I thought they were. I was never without one, either a boyfriend or just a friend. I looked to them to protect me, to help me, and to comfort me. I didn't like being without one. Now, looking back, I can tell that I was making boys a rival to God. For comfort I looked not to God but to the boys he created. And don't think this particular idol didn't break my heart. It did, over and over again. This isn't a statement against dating or having boyfriends. That's all up to you and your parents. All I'm saying is beware your obsession for boys, boys, boys.

Here are some signs you might have a boy idol:

When you are with your friends, all you talk about is boys or a certain boy.

You have or would sneak out and disobey your parents in order to be with him.

You've had or are having sex.

You have the perfect wedding all planned in your head.

You use your body to make him love you.

You usually leave one relationship immediately for another.

If any of these sounds like you, then it's time to get real about the male idols in your life.

Addicted to Love

So fess up, are you "addicted to love"? It's not a cliché for nothing. Love addiction is an actual psychological addiction, and it can be dangerous. If you're a love addict then you know what which I speak. Love is something you long for, wish for, and wait for. You fantasize about it, you dream of it. And you really fear not finding it. And if you have it you'll do all you can to keep it, because after all you'd die without it. You are scared to death of rejection, pain, and being alone forever. If that kinda sounds like you but you're not sure yet, take a look at this list of love addiction symptoms:

Love Addicts:
- are obsessed with thoughts of love
- are scared of change or risk
- lack real intimacy
- manipulate and strike deals to get love
- are overly dependent, clingy
- demand the devotion of the one they love

The Sad Effects of Love Addiction

A surprisingly large number of psychologists have studied people who have an actual addiction to love. To paraphrase a lot of their observations, love addicts are obsessed with finding all they need in another person. They identify themselves by who they are with. They are super proud of their love's look, accomplishments, or success and often take credit for it, as if they had something to do with it. Love addicts are so afraid of change that they do all they can to become indispensable to their bf. Sometimes they are so scared of losing him that they do nothing for themselves. They lose all of their own interests and only focus on what their guy likes. It's like they are nothing without him. Because of this fear they will do anything for their bf. They're just sure that if they can keep them happy then they can keep them. This can lead to all kinds of schemes and plans to keep the relationship going, manipulating their guy and the people around them in order to keep things the same.

The problem is that love addicts are obsessed with a false absolute, believing that they can't live without someone. That's not only false but it's unhealthy, and it hurts both parties involved. When love is your addiction you are not being run by a good emotion but by a self-absorbed one. By making another person responsible for your happiness you squeeze the life out of the relationship and ultimately destroy the very thing you wanted to protect. From a spiritual perspective love addiction turns something like the need for love and attention into a god, and the worship of any god other than the one true God leaves you broken-hearted and bruised. If you are addicted to love then you aren't loving but destroying. Love addiction is something that you must control. And the only way to do that is by choosing to let love go. You have to know that a loss of love won't kill you. You have to choose to love God more than your need for a man. Only when you realign your needs that way will you be able to find true, unconditional love that is blessed by God, and meant for eternity.

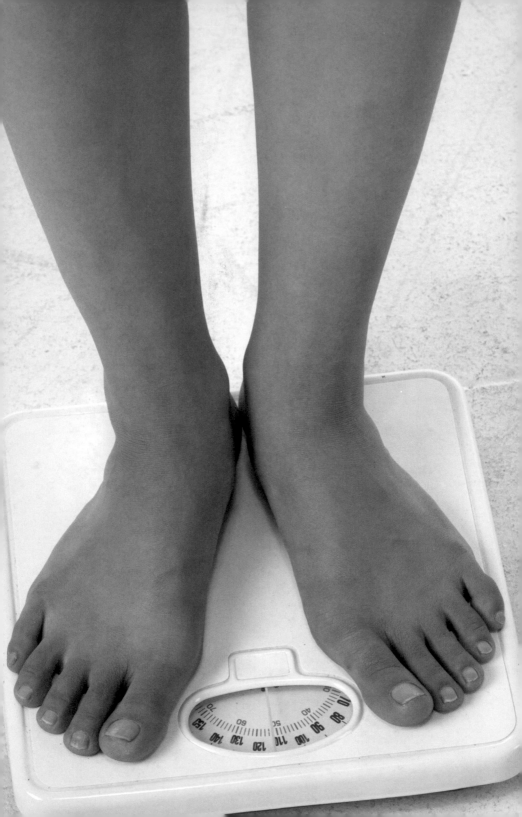

"IT'S ALL ABOUT ME" IDOLS

THE HOT BODY

What's the best way to get a guy's attention? Is it what you say or how you look? If the best way for you is how you look, then you've probably spent a lot of time and energy working on that look. You know just what guys like, and you deliver. You wear the sexiest clothing, the latest fashion, and the sweetest-smelling perfume. And you are perfect. You can't help it if God gave you a sweet little body. If you've got it, flaunt it. Right?

Be careful. Thoughts like this can easily fan the flame of idolatry. You start to rely on your body to get what you want—happiness, attention, relationships. **If your body is your tool for getting what you want, then you might be idolizing the flesh instead of your God.**

THIN IS IN

Okay, if you are obsessed about your weight, you have problems. Do you binge and purge or just avoid every ounce of fat and gram of sugar? What's your technique for keeping yourself looking good? Do you try every new diet out there? Do you cry over how fat you are? Or stare at the mirror and see only blubber while your friends say how skinny you are? If you can't get thin enough, then you are focusing on the wrong thing. Self-obsessions like this lead girls to do stupid things to the very thing they obsess over: themselves. You might not think of getting thin as selfish, but **if you are not overweight but are still obsessed with getting thinner and thinner, you've gone into the land of self-obsession.**

Making yourself your own idol is probably one of the easiest forms of idolatry to fall into. And for girls, worrying over weight is often the entry point into that idolatry. I know weight can be a huge issue, and taking care of your body as the temple of God is a good thing. But getting skinny isn't taking care of the temple; it's abusing the temple. Your body needs—and I don't mean wants but *needs* in the literal sense—nourishment. If you are starving it or depleting it of essential nutrients, you are destroying God's property. If your MySpace page is littered with images of the Olsen twins, Nicole Richie, and Kate Moss and blurbs of "thinspiration," you're living in Idolville. And when you do that it shows that you are living with an entire family of idols, besides just the idol of self. Maybe you idolize being liked or being in control. Or you idolize others and covet what you think they have. Whatever it is, what you are saying to God is, "Your opinion of me doesn't matter as much as _____ (fill in the blank)."

I can't solve all your weight problems right here and now, but what I want you to do, if this sounds like you, is be tough, be smart, and do some research. Get online and find out your body mass index (BMI). This will tell you if your current weight is healthy and normal or not. Then you can go from there. If you are overweight according to the BMI, then you aren't obsessed with being thin, but you might just be obsessed with food. But if you are normal and think they are wrong, you have a huge idol staring you in the face, and it has to be smashed because it's about to smash you. It's survival of the fittest, baby. Who will survive and who will die? It's your choice. Let the idol win or you win. Start the fight now!

What Is Your Ideal Weight?

(WARNING: Math problem ahead!)

Do you know what weight you were made to be? What weight is healthy on you? If you check your BMI, you will know right away if the goal weight you are shooting for is healthy or an ugly obsession. Get online and Google "body mass index" to get a website that will calculate it for you. Or, if you don't have access to a computer and are good with math, here's how to do it yourself: take your weight in pounds and multiply it by 703, then divide it by the square of your height in inches. Don't freak that we're turning your weight into Donald Trump's net worth by multiplying by 703, it's just the formula is a metric one and a lot of you (like me) don't know how many kg we weigh! But both formulas are on the page just in case.

$$\text{BMI} = \frac{\text{(weight in pounds X 703)}}{\text{height in inches}^2}$$

$$\text{BMI} = \frac{\text{(weight in kilograms)}}{\text{height in meters}^2}$$

Reading your BMI results:

Less than 18.5 is underweight (read: too skinny)

18.5–24 is normal

25–29 is overweight

30–39 is obese

40–50 is extremely obese

For more on eating disorders and how to get help, go to www.askhayley.com.

The way to become truly beautiful is by making your thoughts, intentions, and actions look less like yourself and more like Christ.

Hayley DiMarco

WORRY

Worry is a really easy obsession to find yourself with. It's part of your self-protection nerve or something. Worry seems like a valid way to protect yourself, but the truth is that not only is it worthless, it's sinful. **Worry essentially calls God a liar.** He promises to care for you and always be there for you, but for some reason you aren't quite sure that is completely true. Believe me, I know what I'm talking about. Seems like my idols continue to pile up, but it's true: worry is another form of idolatry that I am very prone to. And in the past it's controlled my life. I somehow believed that by worrying really hard about the future, I could make it safer or something. And stopping the worry cycle was the hardest thing I've ever done. But it had to be done.

Do you worry about stuff a lot? Do you get ulcers? Panic attacks? Do you fear the worst and spend all your energy worrying about that worst? Then worry is your god. You trust it more than Yahweh, the true God. I know you don't want to give it up, but facts are facts, and whether you want to or not, worrying has to stop.

> Therefore I tell you, do not worry about your life, what you will eat or drink; or about your body, what you will wear. Is not life more important than food, and the body more important than clothes? Look at the birds of the air; they do not sow or reap or store away in barns, and yet your heavenly Father feeds them. Are you not much more valuable than they? Who of you by worrying can add a single hour to his life? And why do you worry about clothes? See how the lilies of the field grow. They do not labor or spin. Yet I tell you that not even Solomon in all his splendor was dressed like one of these. If that is how God clothes the grass of the field, which is here today and tomorrow is thrown into the fire, will he not much more clothe you, O you of little faith? So do not worry, saying,

"What shall we eat?" or "What shall we drink?" or "What shall we wear?" For the pagans run after all these things, and your heavenly Father knows that you need them. But seek first his kingdom and his righteousness, and all these things will be given to you as well. Therefore do not worry about tomorrow, for tomorrow will worry about itself. Each day has enough trouble of its own.

Matthew 6:25–34

When you worry, it is your personal statement that you don't trust God for your well-being and contentment. And that's insulting to the God who created you. If worry is a habitual thing for you and not just an occasional slip-up, it's time to start smashing and melting that idol.

COMFORT

I've talked a lot about the idol of comfort since it's especially close to my heart (ugh!). If you think you may have an addiction to being comfortable too, here are some things to think about.

You must **struggle against the temptation** to look forward and worry with all your might, for there is no consolation for future troubles promised. And yet, at times, I have found a wonderful consolation even for the future in saying to myself, "Well, it cannot be as I fear unless it is the will of God. And if it is His will then I shall be glad to have it." And this has seemed to hide me in a fortress of peace in reference to this dreaded future.

Hannah Whitall Smith

Comfort can easily become your obsession. Feeling uncomfortable is, well, uncomfortable, and who wants that? So you do all you can to feel good and comfy. You avoid things that make you uncomfortable, so you avoid going certain places, doing certain things, or saying stuff that you should say because it would all make you uncomfortable. Or you are more concerned with how you feel than how others feel because comfort is number one for you and all else takes a distant second or third on your list. Yep, comfort can be an evil taskmaster. Here are some things to think about if you aren't sure if comfort is your idol:

If you are a little cold or your seat is too close to the kitchen when you are in a restaurant, do you complain to the waiter or to your date?

If your friends are having a sleepover, do you whine until you get the bed because you just can't be comfortable on the couch or floor?

If your family was going to do something that made you uncomfortable (like camping), would you say no and stay home instead of going with them?

Do you avoid talking to all strangers (not just the creepy ones) because it's too uncomfortable?

If you were on a reality TV show and you all had to sleep in bunk beds in a big room with no privacy, would you complain because it wasn't comfortable with all those snoring girls around you?

Would you avoid caring for the homeless because you're just too uncomfortable around them?

If you answered yes to any of these, then comfort might be your idol.

The truth is that you were never promised comfort. Believe me, I hate that fact as much as you, but alas, 'tis true. God's Word doesn't include a verse that says, "And the children of God shall find comfort in all they do." Drat! But there are a lot of verses that talk about the opposite of comfort, and that is suffering. Ugh! Hate that! But it's true. So if you think comfort is king, consider some of this stuff:

> For it has been granted to you on behalf of Christ not only to believe on him, but also to suffer for him.
>
> Philippians 1:29

> To this you were called, because Christ suffered for you, leaving you an example, that you should follow in his steps.
>
> 1 Peter 2:21

> For our light and momentary troubles are achieving for us an eternal glory that far outweighs them all.
>
> 2 Corinthians 4:17

> Therefore, since Christ suffered in his body, arm yourselves also with the same attitude, because he who has suffered in his body is done with sin.
>
> 1 Peter 4:1

People like me who seek comfort at all cost, hurt those they love, refuse to help those who need it, and miss out on the trials of life that God offers us in order to perfect us. In my quest to stop worshiping comfort, I have found it helpful to read these verses and find beauty in the trials and the suffering, believing that God allows only the right things to enter my life as long as I am obedient to his Word and trust him with my life.

SELF-HATRED

The Bible tells us that we are to love God and love our neighbors as ourselves. But does it say anything about loving yourself? Well, there are verses about how God loves us and how wonderfully we were made. But technically, those are more about God's character than about our individual value or worth. Still, even though we're sinners, imperfect screwups called to die to self and to be sanctified, words like those don't allow for self-hatred. **If you hate yourself, it's because you have believed a lie of the enemy.** Something someone said or something you heard made you fall into the sin of self-hatred. You might hate your life or the mistakes you have made. You might hate how you look or who you are. But however you cut it, **self-hatred is idolatry. When you hate yourself, you are obsessed.** And whatever caused that obsession, that looking—no, staring—inward has taken your eyes off of God and put them onto you.

If you refuse to believe God's Word when he says how important you are, if you are calling him a liar by discounting his opinion of you, then look out, because you're playing with fire. When you hate yourself, you aren't just hating, you're accusing God of lying. And though you might feel completely safe with self-hatred, I pray you aren't okay with calling the Holy One a big fat liar. Self-hatred says, "I can never be anything of value to anyone." And if you look at it in the right light, it looks a lot like pride—because pride says I'm so special I *should be* perfect. What makes you think that you are so special that you should look perfect, be perfect, and feel perfect? God makes it clear, "There is no one righteous, not even one" (Romans 3:10). Are you calling him a liar by insisting that you *should* be perfect and therefore his Word is wrong? Perhaps you think it should really read, "There is no one righteous because you have failed. If you hadn't failed, I could have written, 'There is only one righteous, and she is sitting right here.'" Look, **you shouldn't be shocked that you aren't perfect. And you shouldn't hate that fact because God doesn't hate it; he expects it.** There is truly only one perfect person, and his name is Jesus. So you shouldn't be shocked that you have failed, have messed up, or are just not good enough. No duh! None of us are. None! So get over it and believe God's Word. You are good enough if you simply trust him. Simply because you believe. No other act is required in order for you to be loved by him. Simply believe and you are in. Even the apostle Paul, while calling himself the greatest sinner of all, didn't hate himself. That would have been self-centered. Instead, he said to boast about your weaknesses (see the verses below).

If you hate yourself, then please, please, my love, read these verses. They are directly from God's mouth to your eyes. He loves you very, very much. And he wants you to see things his way. Love the only perfect one and forget about how imperfect you are. Look upward instead of inward. And believe.

> As it is written: "There is no one righteous, not even one."
>
> Romans 3:10

> If you confess with your mouth, "Jesus is Lord," and believe in your heart that God raised him from the dead, you will be saved.
>
> Romans 10:9

> But he said to me, "My grace is sufficient for you, for my power is made perfect in weakness." Therefore I will boast all the more gladly about my weaknesses, so that Christ's power may rest on me.
>
> 2 Corinthians 12:9

> Blessed are the poor in spirit, for theirs is the kingdom of heaven.
>
> Matthew 5:3

Consider it pure joy, my brothers, whenever you face trials of many kinds, because you know that the testing of your faith develops perseverance. Perseverance must finish its work so that you may be mature and complete, not lacking anything.

James 1:2–4

The LORD your God is with you, he is mighty to save. He will take great delight in you, he will quiet you with his love, he will rejoice over you with singing.

Zephaniah 3:17

Take my yoke upon you and learn from me, for I am gentle and humble in heart, and you will find rest for your souls.

Matthew 11:29

Let your trials, your shortcomings, your tragedies be a reason to get on your knees and worship God, not a reason to focus inward and worship yourself. Don't lick your wounds and remember how awful things are; focus on the God you serve and the love he has for you. When you do that, all the self-hatred and suffering will lift right off your shoulders.

If through a broken heart God can bring His purposes to pass in the world, then thank Him for breaking your heart.

Oswald Chambers

FEAR

God calls us not to fear, so **fear is already a sin. It questions God's faithfulness.** But **when it runs your life, it becomes an idol too.** It's like this: you become a slave to fear when you act because of it. Take the fear of flying as an example. Let's say you're totally afraid of flying. That fear isn't necessarily an idol. It's unfounded, since flying is safer than driving, but it's not an idol until it controls your life. And that happens something like this: let's say you have a family member in another state who seriously needs you right away. They ask you to fly out tonight to come help them. But you are too afraid of flying, so you tell them you can't come. That's proof that fear is controlling your life.

I *am* afraid of flying. I seriously hate it. But I fly all over the place, because I refuse to let fear become my god. Now, I'm not saying it's easy; it's been really rough at times, but the more I learn to trust God with my life, the less fear has a grip on me. And the truth is, the more I realize that fear is an idol, the more I want to stand up to it. Remember, courage isn't having no fear; it's being afraid but doing what scares you anyway. Be courageous!

If I can do it, I know you can too. Don't let fear tell you what to do. Fear is just the enemy's attempt to lie to you about who God is. A lot of times fear is sort of inherited. Like how I got a lot of my fears from watching my mom. If you want a great book on tackling fear to recommend to a parent or other adult, my husband Michael wrote one that rocks called *All In: Gambling on Life, Love, and Faith in a World of Risk.*

> For you did not receive a spirit that makes you a slave again to fear, but you received the Spirit of sonship. And by him we cry, "Abba, Father."
>
> Romans 8:15

Be strong and courageous. Do not fear or be in dread of them, for it is the LORD your God who goes with you. He will not leave you or forsake you.

Deuteronomy 31:6 ESV

GODLY IDOLS?

VOWS OF SELF-PROTECTION

Have you ever promised yourself or God that you would never do a certain thing again because you were hurt by it once? Sometimes that's a good thing, like when you were disobedient and now are promising not to do that wrong thing again. But **sometimes when you swear never to let something happen to you again, you could be making that oath your idol.** When what you want or don't want becomes more of an obsession than what God wants or doesn't want, it becomes your idol. For example, God never promised you that you would never be hurt or heartbroken. If you vow never to be hurt again, then you want something that God doesn't necessarily promise. So if you were hurt really bad by your dad and you promise never to trust another man again as long as you live, you make that oath your idol. You close your thoughts and mind to all that God might put in front of you if it looks like it will interfere with your pledge. You refuse gifts, opportunities, and even trials that God wants to put you through in order to draw you nearer to him.

I can remember when I was a girl and my dad left my mom and me. I was devastated. My mom was too. And as I watched her fall apart emotionally, I decided that I would never let that happen to either of us again, and so I vowed to never act like a girl again but to "be a man." Not in the I-want-to-be-a-boy kind of way, but in an emotionally distant, tough, I-can-do-it-all-on-my-own kind of way that a lot of girls of divorce create for themselves. Over my lifetime this vow I made plagued me. Every relationship I had with a guy ended in heartache because I was unwilling to be who God created me to be and unwilling to accept the gifts that God put in my path. It wasn't until I renounced that vow

to myself and determined to trust *God* with my love life and let him direct my steps that I became free to love and to find the man of my life. The perfect man for me.

It's time to learn that you can't completely protect yourself from heartache or emotional trials. In fact, the more you try to protect yourself from pain, the more pain you will get into. And check this out: making vows for self-protection can show that you don't really get God's Word because his Word promises that *he* will protect you and shows that all you have to do is obey his law and trust that even awful stuff is allowed to happen because it is important and will ultimately make your life better. Getting this concept and trusting God is the only thing that will give you peace and awesome hope that your Lord will meet all your needs.

> And we know that in all things God works for the good of those who love him, who have been called according to his purpose.
>
> Romans 8:28

When **what you want** or don't want becomes more of an **obsession** than what **God wants** or doesn't want, it becomes your idol.

A Truly Godly Vow

Vows made to God for the right purpose are truly godly. Here is the definition of a godly vow. The purpose of a vow is to get favor from God, to show him how thankful you are for something he did for you, or just to prove to him that you are absolutely devoted to him by abstaining from something.* A vow becomes sinful when it has no correlation to a biblical mandate or command and isn't a promise to God made in order to draw yourself closer to him.

*Definition paraphrased from Walter A. Elwell and Philip Wesley Comfort, *Tyndale Bible Dictionary*, Tyndale Reference Library (Wheaton: Tyndale, 2001), 1288.

GOD'S WILL

Have you ever wanted to know God's will so badly that you made a deal with him? "I'll do A if you'll do B first." In other words, it might go something like this: "I'll know for sure that you want me to go to Zimbabwe to help the orphans if you make it so that my bff can go with me." It's a great thing to search for God's will, but **when your deals with him become the way to find your way around life, then you have to beware, because you might just be testing God.** Is he listening? I'll run a test and see. Is he truly trustworthy? Let me put him to the test to find out. **Waiting for God to prove himself to you before you obey his Word is an idolatry of its own.** "We should not test the Lord, as some of them did—and were killed by snakes" (1 Corinthians 10:9).

Testing God is not an idol that you deliberately chose as a rival to God, but instead you probably truly believed it was a way to get to the point of serving him. You had good intentions, but you might want to rethink your way of obedience. All you really need to know of God's will in order to act is his Word. It has all that you need in order to make decisions about serving and obeying him. Here's a little Hayley story: One time I was trying to decide between two jobs. I was offered one in Hawaii, starting a new church, and one in Nashville at a publishing house. I really wanted Nashville but felt like I should probably choose Hawaii because it seemed more like serving God. When I was struggling with the decision, a pastor helped me out by telling me this analogy. Since my motivations were pure in going to either place, it was like Hawaii is the swing set and Nashville is the teeter-totter. You can choose either one—just stay on the playground, that's all God asks. Choose whichever you want. See, neither was against God's Word, so neither was a sin. I decided to do what I wanted and move to Nashville. And now I

know for certain it was exactly what I should have done. It's what led me to the publishing world and ultimately to writing books like this. I'm so glad that I didn't wait for a sign from God or choose what looked like the more "holy" option. God's Word gives us the boundaries of the playground we can play on, and choosing which thing to do is up to us.

ADDICTION ANYONE?

The National Institute on Drug Abuse defines substance dependence as a disorder characterized by criteria that include the following:

spending a great deal of time using the substance

using it more often than one intends

thinking about reducing use or making repeated unsuccessful efforts to reduce use

giving up important social, family, or occupational activities to use it

reporting withdrawal symptoms when one stops using it

avoidance of quitting because of withdrawals

If you can relate to at least three of these, then you might just be addicted. But you don't use drugs, so what does this have to do with anything? Well, you're probably quick enough to notice that this addiction thing looks an awful lot like obsession. And you'd be right. Congratulations! Now the question is, what are you addicted to? When it comes to any of the following, do you have an addiction?

FOOD

Food is probably one of the biggest idols in the world. How many times have women resorted to a pint of ice cream and a spoon in order to take the sting off of a really bad day? How many people die each year of food-related illnesses? Food is intoxicating and amazing. But it can easily become an idol if you aren't careful. I can remember when I worked in an office where I didn't really like my job. The only way I got through the day was by thinking about what I was going to eat when I got home. I survived because I got to eat what I liked. When I was in college in Europe, I gained a ton of weight because I was super lonely and chocolate mousse was my bff. It would take away the loneliness, at least for the few minutes it took to eat it. Yes, I can say that food can easily be my idol if I let it.

How about you? Do you love food—I mean really, really love it? Can you control it or does it control you? Who's in charge? Here's a way to find out. **For the next week I dare you to only eat what you hate.** Yep, that's right, don't eat anything you love, like desserts or bread. No Coke or coffee. Just stuff that's good for you like broccoli, asparagus, and other vegetables. Don't put on any fancy, yummy sauces; just eat it raw. Eat like you're on *Survivor* and you don't have access to any fire. Eat salad without dressing; eat stuff that just doesn't do it for you. Or how about liver and onions? Can you do it? If you say no way, then food sounds like the boss of you.

Do you worship food or the feeling it gives you? Does your body prove it? Are you unhealthy? Walk away from the idol of food. Do it now, or it might one day take your life.

Remember, **ask yourself if at least three of the criteria for addiction listed above fit you when it comes to food.** It can help you to really get eating into perspective. **Are you addicted?**

TV

What's your favorite show? Does it just kill you to miss it? Would you say that you were addicted? In psychological studies, **people who watched a lot of TV reported feeling like the energy was just sucked out of them after long bouts of watching television.** TV keeps you relaxed and sedentary. It can feel like a great way to unwind, but it can also keep you depressed, inactive, and disinterested in life. If you think you might have a TV addiction, take this quick quiz to find out.

Do you have a TV in your bedroom?

Do you watch more than two hours of TV a day?

Do you run your life around your shows?

Do you eat dinner in front of the TV?

Can you tell me what time it is by what's on the TV?

Do you have to have the TV on to fall asleep or to unwind before bed?

Do you feel like you watch too much TV?

Do you ever watch more TV at one time than you planned?

Can you turn off your favorite show in the middle of it?

Have you ever missed an important family or other event because of TV?

Does you TiVo have more than ten Season Passes?

If you answered yes to three of these, then you might have an addiction. If you answered yes to four to six of these, then look out TV Addicts Anonymous, there's a new member in town. Answering yes to almost all of these makes you a TV junkie. So how does it feel? Do you realize that being *that* obsessed with TV can wreck havoc with your life? It can make you depressed, lonely, and despondent. Because of TV you can avoid exercise, social functions, and reality.

TV can tug at you like every other idol—trouble is, it is such a socially accepted, even encouraged, idol. Lots of people make it the focus of conversation when they get together with friends. Rather than living their own lives, they live vicariously through the lives of actors and screenwriters.

TV in and of itself isn't evil. You can learn a lot of things by watching TV, but if you are addicted to TV, then TV has become your idol. It's like a drug that you take in order to feel something different than what you are feeling before you watch it. And just like a drug, it can have nasty withdrawal symptoms. And that's what keeps you from stopping—fear of withdrawals. But it's time to risk it. The withdrawals won't last forever. Letting go of an idol like TV not only will give you more time for things that are good for you, like exercise, but also will give you more time to get to know your God.

If any of these addiction symptoms fit your relationship with TV, then you have an idol:

You spend a great deal of time watching TV.

You watch it more often than you planned a lot of the time.

You've thought about not watching so much, and even tried to cut back, but failed.

You've missed important social or family activities to watch.

You've experienced withdrawal symptoms when you stopped watching it.

You avoid quitting because of the pain you think quitting will cause.

Is TV one of your rivals to God? Know yourself, know your TV, and get rid of your idols.

CELL PHONE

The *Taipei Times*, a paper I'm sure you never miss reading, says **cell phone addiction might be one of the biggest non-drug addictions in the twenty-first century.** Wow! How do you feel about your cell phone? Is it ever out of your reach? Do you feel anxious when you don't have it with you? Do your parents think you're out of control? Spotting a cell addiction isn't too tough. In fact, you probably know if you are addicted without any further probing. But I want you to understand that this isn't some kind of safe, godly addiction to have. Remember, **there are no godly addictions or obsessions other than God himself. So if you call yourself a phone addict, you've got an idol to deal with.**

The cell isn't evil in and of itself. So I'm not suggesting you ditch it completely. It can be a good safety precaution and a good way to keep in touch with your parents when you're away from home. But just like those other "light" idols, it needs to be managed. Here are some ways to control your cell and take away its idol status:

Never have a conversation longer than five minutes.

Don't use your cell more than a half hour per day. (A cell phone addict is defined as someone who feels a need to use it more than a half hour per day.*)

* Sydney morning herald, http://www.smh.com.au/articles /2003/12/10/1070732250532.html?from=storyrhs

Don't take it with you to class. It's disrespectful to your teacher and the other students, as if you think your calls are more important than school. It makes you look selfish, not godly.

Turn it off except when you really need it or your parents might need to get in touch with you.

Don't carry it on your belt or hold it in your hand while you walk around the mall or at the gym.

Don't look at it every time it rings as if the most important thing in the world is to see who is calling. That just reeks of worship.

Don't have it on during mealtimes. Show the people you are eating with that they are important to you.

Don't interrupt conversations with your friends to answer the phone unless it's your parents or another important person—i.e., not just another friend who wants to chat. When you do that it's rude and shows everyone that your phone is your idol. And being rude is caring more for yourself than others. That's the opposite of dying to self.

Never talk on it in a restaurant, in a class, or in the library. It's rude.

Make talking in person more important than texting or talking on the phone.

Manage your minutes—never go over! Going over means you are a slave to your phone. It has become your master, and as God's Word says, you can't serve two masters (see Luke 16:13). Choose: God or the cell phone.

You only need one cell phone. If you have more than one, you are a glutton.

Are You a Glutton?

Gluttony doesn't have to be just something related to food. Are you a glutton when it comes to *things*? How many cells do you own? How many pairs of shoes? Don't be a glutton (see Philippians 3:19). Gluttony is a sign of idolatry. Find your excess and find your idol.

GAMING

I love The Sims. There was a time when I could play it for hours. I especially loved learning the cheats so I could give myself a bunch of money and then build a huge house and furnish it. I was getting addicted. Luckily I just don't have the time to play it anymore or I'd probably still be going on it. Computer games are amazing. They can be a total escape from life, giving you a virtual life right in front of you. Are you a gamer? Do you own an Xbox, PlayStation, or Nintendo? Or do you prefer an online community like Second Life? There's nothing wrong with gaming to a certain extent, but once it becomes your obsession, strange things can happen. If gaming is your obsession (read: idol), it's like you have become your own god, designing your own world that you feel is far better than the real one God has given you. **If you aren't sure if gaming is an obsession or just a fun pastime, then consider these questions:**

Do games help you to escape from life?

Do you feel better when you're playing?

Is your online life more important than your real life?

Do you play more than one hour per day?

Do you spend most of your non-school hours playing?

Do you fall asleep in school?

Are your grades getting worse?

Are you irritable, angry, or depressed when you aren't playing?

Have you lied about using your computer or playing games?

Do you feel guilty about playing video games?

Do you get headaches, backaches, and dry eyes because you play so much?

Do you see what I see when I look at this list? Video games sound just like a jealous god that demands you spend time with him and gets very nasty when you don't. It causes you to feel depressed, angry, even sick if you neglect it. The idol of gaming is a vicious god who doesn't want to let you go. It's time to decide now who you will serve—your video god or the one true God. The choice is yours, and you have to live with the consequences. So choose wisely.

INTERNET

What did people do before the Internet? I mean, it has everything. All the facts, fun, and relationships you could want, all in one place, at your fingertips. The Internet has become an essential part of life. I know I would be hard-pressed to work without it. But just like every other good thing in the world, the Internet can become an obsession. So what's it like for you? Do you have an Internet addiction? Just like any other drug or addictive substance, the Internet can draw you in and hook you. And suddenly **you feel like you can't live without it. You think about it all day.** You get on it whenever humanly possible, and you even dream about it. If the Internet has you by the fingertips, then it's time to free your digits from that keyboard. Not permanently, but let's give it a breather. Otherwise you'll be serving the World Wide Web like it's an ugly slave master. Just like a gaming addiction, Internet addiction has some telltale signs that show you who's boss in your life right now. Is it you or the W³?

Does the Internet help you to escape from life?
Do you feel better when you're on it?
Is your online life more important than your real life?
Do you surf more than one hour per day?
Do you spend most of your non-school hours surfing?
Do you fall asleep in school?
Are your grades getting worse?
Are you irritable, angry, or depressed when you aren't online?
Have you lied about using your computer?
Do you feel guilty about being online so much?
Do you get headaches, backaches, and dry eyes because you are online so much?

Notice how the Internet is a cruel god who wants all your allegiance and time, just like gaming. He wants you to sacrifice all just to serve him. It's not something to take lightly; the idol you have served has to be dethroned. But just like the other light idols, it's one you'll have to learn to manage. There will be times when you will need the Internet for study or work, so you'll have to get control back in your life so that the Net doesn't try to control you. So here are some ideas:

Cut back your time online to one hour per day, unless your classes or work require more.
Move the computer out of your room.
Get out of the house and get some exercise.
Read books, talk to friends, hang out with your family.
Have an adult hold you accountable.

Clinic for Internet Addiction

In March 2005 a government clinic for Internet addiction was opened at the Beijing Military Region Central Hospital in the People's Republic of China. It treats patients, mostly youths between the ages of fourteen and twenty-four, who suffer from anxiety, depression, and lack of sleep, often due to long hours on online video games and chats. Treatments include Internet "cold turkey," counseling, physical activity, antidepressants, and enforcement of strict regular sleeping patterns.

Source: Wired News, "Beijing Clinic Treats Web Addicts," July 3, 2005, http://www.wired.com/news/culture/0,1284,68081,00.html.

PLEASING PEOPLE

Are you a people pleaser? It sounds like a nice thing—you care about people, maybe more than you should, and it gets you into trouble? Most people pleasers think they are just overly caring, and caring's a good thing, but the people they care for abuse that, and that's when things go bad. But what if it isn't their fault at all but is the fault of an idol? **If pleasing people is your obsession, then you are bound for disappointment, because as they say, you can please some of the people some of the time, but you can't please all of the people all of the time.** So you are pursuing a futile task. You can never please them. And the fact of the matter is, if your main goal is to please people, then it is no longer your main goal to please God. God's Word talks specifically about this when it says, "For am I now seeking the approval of man, or of God? Or am I trying to please man? If I were still trying to please man, I would not be a servant of Christ" (Galatians 1:10 ESV). Paul asks himself a question and gives himself the answer. Being a people pleaser isn't a noble title. In fact, it's a dangerous one.

God isn't unable to help us, and He doesn't despise us. He is the ruler of all mankind and the lover of His own people. But through suffering He looks into and searches everyone. He weighs the character of every individual during danger, even death. Therefore, as God is revealed in the fire, so our true selves are revealed in critical moments.

Minucius Felix

If you have any area in your life where your main goal is to impress or please people, then you have misplaced your allegiance, and trouble is bound to be the result. It's not bad to serve others and to care for them, but sometimes serving them and caring for them might mean not pleasing them. Like when a baby wants nothing but sugar to eat—you can't please them and just give them what they want, because that wouldn't be caring for them. So if you're a people pleaser, move your focus off of the people and onto your God. He might have trials and difficulties planned for them that you are working hard to relieve. Or he might want someone else to help them. People pleasers are really more obsessed with getting approval and love than with serving others in obedience to God. So check your motives: what do you want or need from people? And then stop blaming others for your idol of people pleasing.

SUMMING IT ALL UP

We all have plenty of idols to choose from, and most of us have more than one. I'll bet you didn't know the idols that were in your life, but now that you do, I hope you want to see a change. Change can come, and it will come if you will trust God's Word and be fearless about following it. Idols seem to be a natural part of human nature, a result of satisfying the flesh, so don't condemn yourself or hate yourself for them—just get real with yourself. You are human and you have sinned, but there is forgiveness. God wants you to bring your heart back home and to remember your love for him. His forgiveness comes easy—all you have to do is confess your sin and accept his forgiveness. So if you are willing to call an idol an idol and to move on toward healing and faithfulness, then let's do just that and get idol free.

"Living idol free
will mean a lot of
change is about to
start in your life."
Hayley DiMarco

chapter 4

IDOL FREE

Enter by the narrow gate.

For the gate is wide and the way is easy that leads to destruction, and those who enter by it are many. For the gate is narrow and the way is hard that leads to life, and those who find it are few.

Matthew 7:13–14 ESV

Living idol free will mean a lot of change is about to start in your life. When you've had something in your life for so long, getting rid of it can be really hard and painful, but the results will be amazing. You will find true happiness and peace, your hope will be restored, and your relationship with God will flourish. So let's work together to kick the butts of these nasty idols and draw closer to the true God.

Here are some things that will help you spot all the idols in your life and then break them.

LISTEN TO THE HOLY SPIRIT

The first step in becoming idol free is to find out who or what your idols are, which we kinda have been doing for like 142 pages. But I'm not gonna pretend I don't know how the mind of an idolater works, because I do—I have one. And the internal conversation can go something like this: "This *could* be an idol, but it's not *really* that bad, so maybe it's not. I mean, I don't want to be a wacko or anything. I'm not hurting anyone and I *can* control myself, so it's probably not an idol." Been there, done that. So I know that of which I speak. **Don't let your mind lie to you and change the subject to something happier. Let's get to the root of these idols and tear them out.**

It helps to have someone in your corner, besides me, and you actually already have someone else. This friend is better than any other source, 'cuz he gets right to the heart of the matter and won't let you lie to yourself about your obsessions. His name? The Holy Spirit. (Okay, guess I gave that away in the section title, but it flows, huh?)

When Jesus was getting all ready to leave the earth, he told his gang about the Holy Spirit: *"And I will ask the Father, and he will give you another Counselor to be with you forever"* (John 14:16).

And it sounds pretty cool, doesn't it? A full-time counselor who is always with you. Always ready to help you get better and find your idols. I've been to a few counselors over my lifetime, and frankly, they haven't done near as much for me as my personal counselor, the H.S. But the key is listening. You gotta listen.

Plain and simple, **the Holy Spirit is your connection to God the Father.** He's the one that helps you to hear and understand the truth. That's one of the reasons Jesus called him a counselor. But the Holy Spirit also has another very important job, and this is the one that will come in handy for you in getting idol free. Check it out:

> And He [the Holy Spirit], when He comes, will convict the world concerning sin and righteousness and judgment; concerning sin, because they do not believe in Me; and concerning righteousness, because I go to the Father and you no longer see Me; and concerning judgment, because the ruler of this world has been judged.
>
> John 16:8–11 NASB

This verse says that one of the jobs of the Holy Spirit is to convict you. That means that if you still aren't convinced of all your idols, the Holy Spirit can help you out. **Think about your list of potential obsessions and ask God, through his Holy Spirit, to convict you so you can know for sure what's an idol and what's not.**

CONFESS

Okay, an obsession is an idol, right? We've gotten that much, but you might not have caught the note about an idol looking a lot like an addiction. **To be addicted is "to devote or surrender (oneself) to something habitually or obsessively"** (e.g., addicted to shopping), according to Webster's Dictionary. Sounds a lot like an idol, doesn't it? And just like drug addicts and alcoholics facing their addictions, the first thing you have to do with an idol is admit that you have a problem. **Part of admitting your idol problem, as a believer, is agreeing with God that you have a problem, and that's called confession.** Confession is good for the soul and is the first step in getting back to your true God.

Confessing isn't all that hard. All you have to do is talk to God. Talk to him like you would talk to me. Talk to him like a friend. Admit what you've been doing and loving is wrong and tell him you want to change. Simple. So make confession the first action step in becoming idol free.

We need to cultivate in our own hearts the same hatred of sin God has. Hatred of sin as sin, not just as something disquieting or defeating to ourselves, but as displeasing to God, lies at the root of all holiness.

Jerry Bridges

PRAY

Another way to shatter your idols is to spend time with the true God. Your God. The Holy One. The Alpha and the Omega, the beginning and the end. Prayer can seem like such a mundane task. It can oftentimes turn into a chance to ask for food for your idols. "Please give me this," and "Help me make this happen," and "Blah, blah, blah." And that's tragic. So I suggest you avoid the asking altogether for a while and just stick to adoring and thanking. Talk to God about how wonderful he is and how much you love him and need him. Confess. Promise. And love on him. Spend time in his presence praising him. Pray to him in song and worship. Entire books have been written on the subject of prayer, and this isn't one of them. So if you need help getting into prayer more, find a good book. Ask around. Do what you can to learn more. It really is communion with God, and it will change your life. Don't let it be a struggle anymore; get the tools you need to get back on your knees and away from your idols. Prayer will help you to break the bonds that tie you.

I know I said to keep it all about God, but before you get to that, the prayer that needs to take place is the prayer of confession and repentance. And now would be a good time to pray it. So talk to God and tell him the idols you have discovered. Thank him for showing them to you and for understanding that you didn't realize what you were doing. Also call them a sin, and then thank him for the forgiveness of sins. Then ask him for the help to be free from your idols, and tell him of your repentance. If you haven't already, then take some time right now to talk to him, and then at the end of it I want you to sign this agreement.

Dear God, I thank you for listening to me and for forgiving me. Now I want to tell you right here and now that I am going to walk away and never return to the following idols:

_____

_____

_____

_____

_____

_____

_____

_____

Thank you, God, for your love. I promise to turn from these idols and to worship only you.

_____

(sign your name here)

PLEASE DON'T FEED THE IDOLS

Idols are like nasty pets that you've coddled and cuddled for so long that they don't want to leave. They're all mangy, nasty, fat, and rabid. And you want to get rid of them now. Like with any other unwanted animal, you can be mean to them, tell them you don't want them anymore, and yell at them to go away, but until you stop feeding them, they are going to continue to claw at your door. I would bet that you've been feeding your idols since you were a kid and they've gotten really used to coming to you for nourishment, so getting rid of them will mean stopping the food supply.

So the next question is, **what is the food supply to your particular idol? Food is anything that makes them grow, comforts them, or encourages them to stick around.** And it goes like this. If shopping is my idol, then one way to feed that idol is to read tons of magazines and watch *What Not to Wear*. The more you do these things, the more you grow your idol. Idol food is like potato chips. It's hard to stop with just one. Once your little idol buddy gets a taste of food, instead of being satisfied, he wants more. In fact, he never gets enough food. And the more you give him, the bigger he gets and the more powerful he is in your life.

If your idol is shopping, or being cute, or being perfectly dressed, and you read magazines and study fashion, you are not only feeding your idol but worshiping him. It's like bringing a food offering to the altar of your idol. And it says to the idol and everyone watching that the idol is the most important thing in your life. And practically speaking, it becomes true. The more you feed him, the worse it gets.

So please, **please don't feed the idols. If you want to obey God and destroy your idols, it's time to starve them.** Just in case you don't know what idol food is, let's have a look at some idol delicacies.

MAGAZINES

Magazines are great. I have like seven subscriptions to mags. They are so quick and easy to get information from, and they are a great way to spend some downtime. But magazines have a dangerous side too. And that is that they can be idol food. See, **when you look at a magazine that feeds your particular idol, it reminds you of what you love but don't have.** In the name of "learning more" about your favorite thing, like clothes, video games, or movie stars, magazines draw you deeper and deeper into your obsession. They keep your mind, heart, and soul focused on the rival that is attempting to take over God's position in your life.

Here's one really easy way to tell if your favorite magazine is feeding your idolatrous habit. **After you read it, do you feel bummed a little because you don't have the newest whatsit or thingamabob?** Do you start to yearn deep down in your heart for that perfect thing you read about between the pages? Do you look at the things you already have and start to daydream about getting rid of them and replacing them with the newest and latest version of them? **If your magazines keep you thinking about, pining over, or daydreaming of your obsession, then it's time to tear down your idols and tear up the pages.** Stop the subscriptions; turn your

head when you see them at the checkout stand. Wipe every bit of idol food off your fingers and keep it that way. Magazines can really drive a wedge between you and God and cause you much more grief than you ever imagined if they are food for your idols.

MUSIC

Music is good for the soul. Lots of people say it is the number one way that they commune with God. And good worship music can take away your depression and lift your heart up into the clouds. But not all "worship music" is directed at God. Lots of music is made to worship other things, like love, boys, romance, and everything related to things you don't have. **If the music you listen to has you daydreaming about your wish list or the things you used to think you "need" to survive, then it's definitely idol food.**

Remember earlier in the book when I talked about emo (p. 40)? My emo before there was an emo phase all revolved around music. One time during a really depressing part of my life, I used to love to get into the tub, light a bunch of candles, and play really sad, romantic music. I would listen and cry and cry over the love I didn't have or the love I had just lost. I thought it was cleansing. But I was wrong. Instead of helping me to move on and get over my lost love, it only made things worse. It made me dream of what I didn't have. It made me feel resentful that I didn't have it, and it drove me away from God. So check out the music you listen to and see what it does to your thoughts.

MOVIES/TV

TV and movies can be superidol delicacies as well. Idols can even be voted on and made by the people watching their TV. In fact, for some people certain shows can even become their idols. I don't want to sound like a broken record, so let me point you back to what I said about music, because the same thing applies to movies and TV. But in this case it can be compounded. Not only do you get drawn into idol worship of things, people, and ideas that you crave but you can also start to worship actors and actresses.

Do you have a movie star as an idol? Do you have their pictures all over your wall or MySpace profile? Do you talk about them all the time? Daydream about meeting them? When I was in high school I had a huge crush on a singer/soap opera star named Rick Springfield. You know, the guy who sang "Jessie's Girl"? I and many other girls just knew that one day we would meet him and he would fall in love with us. My best friend at the time felt the same way. I can remember the last time we ever talked. It was a conversation about Rick Springfield. I told her I was in love with him and wanted to marry him. She got really mad at me and told me I couldn't because *she* was going to marry him. She got so mad that she kicked me out of her house, and that was that. No more friendship, all because I threatened to take away her idol. Ha! True story!

Watching TV or movies is a great pastime, and I admit I watch my fair share. I love reality shows because I love studying how people act and react in certain situations and it keeps me in touch with what society and the media are feeding us all. But it can also easily feed my appetite for idols. Especially the ads. Ads can get you to crave all kinds of things; that's why I fast-forward past them all with my TiVo. Just a way to avoid feeding my idols.

If you feel more attached to your idols after watching a particular show, then never again. Stop watching it immediately. Don't let entertainment feed your idol. And if entertainment itself is your idol, then look out. It's time to get rid of the old TV set and stereo.

According to one study, "Girls aged between 14 and 16 who tended to obsess over a particular celebrity **were also less happy** with their own body image and tried to change the way they looked."

Richard Gray, "Teen Idols 'Help Youths Move into Adulthood,'" Scotsman.com, March 5, 2006, http://news.scotsman.com/scitech.cfm?id=333862006.

BOOKS

I'm a book freak. I love books. I own like thousands of them and I keep buying more. I really, really enjoy them. And there is nothing wrong with that for me, because I'm not consuming books that feed my idols. For instance, I don't buy romance novels because I know they would affect me. But if what you are reading is feeding your idols, then it's time to stop reading the books you love and break away from the claws of the enemy.

For many girls romance novels are huge idol foods. They feed their appetite for the perfect man and cause them to covet the dreamy guy in the pages of the book. I talk about this a lot in my other books, so bear with me, but I think it's a huge issue for us girls. Romance novels feed your appetite for romance. And while romance is wonderful and exciting, it can become a very evil taskmaster, making you feel awful because you don't have it. I can remember reading a romance novel and feeling my blood rush to my face with excitement. I would dream of the scene I was reading and fantasize about being in it myself. This fantasy was like a silent prayer to God, saying, "My life is miserable, and what you've given me isn't enough. I want more; I must have more; I will die without more." And I coveted perfect romance. If you covet the dream guy, if you salivate over romance, if you get depressed after reading a book because you are alone in your room in your romanceless little life with no hope for love . . . then stop reading romance novels!

Maybe your idol is not romance but escape from reality or dwelling on dark, depressing thoughts. Whatever it is, if it's found in your books, you've gotta get rid of them. They are feeding the idol you want to shatter. Don't you see that if what you are doing brings your idol more and more to the front of your mind, then it has to be stopped and stopped immediately?

FRIENDS

Friends can also be idol feeders. Not all friends are helping you to remain an idolater, but some just might be keeping you looking in the wrong direction for God. When you look at the idol list that you've come up with so far, **can you think of any friends of yours who share your idols or who really drive you to your idols?** You might have a friend who is really a "things" freak. She has to have the latest this or the latest that, and she expects you to have the same. If being around her makes you crave pleasing and feeding your idol, then some changes have to happen. I'm not suggesting immediately dumping her as a friend, but if you talk to her and get her this book to go through and she still refuses to forsake her idol, then you have to move on. You can't let her sin drag you down. God has counsel on such matters, and here is some that might help you:

> As for a person who stirs up division, after warning him once and then twice, have nothing more to do with him, knowing that such a person is warped and sinful; he is self-condemned.
>
> Titus 3:10–11 ESV

If you talk to her and she still continues to argue with you about her idol of choice, then it is plain as day here: have nothing more to do with her. When believers are confronted with their sin and refuse to repent from it, especially when they are dragging you down with them, it's time to move on. Otherwise you will continue to worship your idols instead of God.

> For you may be sure of this, that everyone who is sexually immoral or impure, or who is covetous (that is, <u>an idolater</u>), has no inheritance in the kingdom of Christ and God. <u>Let no one deceive you with empty words</u>, for because of these things the wrath of God comes upon the sons of disobedience. Therefore <u>do not associate with them</u>; for at one time you were darkness, but now you are light in the Lord. Walk as children of light.
>
> Ephesians 5:5–8 ESV

Before you figured out you had idols, you were in darkness, but now you are in the light. What are you going to do about it? If you keep hanging out with her, then you will remain in darkness. And God wants you to stay in the light. So it might be time to choose. If she is a bad influence, then she's a bad friend.

I know this sounds really harsh, like I'm asking you to live the life of a sequestered nun or something, but I'm not. I'm just saying **you need to know your weaknesses for idolatry and avoid the things that draw you back into it.** There are a lot of other things in this world that can occupy your time. Until right now you probably didn't know that the things you were doing were helping you to worship your idol, but now that you do, you have to make a choice. Will you turn a blind eye and pretend you haven't seen or read what you've seen and read? Or will you start today to make a change? I know it seems hard. I know you love your idols; that's only natural. But it's time to hate them. It's time to think like God and act like Jesus and take up your cross. It can be done. Others around the world are doing it with you. And God is present for every move you make. He has given you the strength to deny your passions, your desires, and your obsessions. It's all at your fingertips; you just have to choose to do it.

So if you're still up for the fight, let's keep on checking out the tools that will help you break up your idols and smash them to the ground.

BE THANKFUL

The next weapon in your arsenal against idols is thankfulness. God created this great tool to help you stay focused on him and his gifts and to draw your eyes and mind off of the enemy and his fake gods. Giving thanks helps you clear your mind of negative, idolatrous thoughts and bring it back onto your God. But for some, being thankful can seem like an impossible chore. When you are engulfed in idols, thankfulness is usually the furthest thing from your mind. So how do you do it? How do you get thankful and get God back into your sights? It's really easy, actually. It just takes repetition. Your mind believes whatever you tell it or show it most often. If you want to be happy, joyful, and peaceful, then focus on those kinds of things. As the apostle Paul says, "*Finally, brothers, whatever is true, whatever is honorable, whatever is just, whatever is pure, whatever is lovely, whatever is commendable, if there is any excellence, if there is anything worthy of praise, think about these things*" (Philippians 4:8 ESV). So let's work at doing just that.

I love this exercise, and I tell people about it all the time. So if you've already heard it, forgive me. But it works wonderfully. Get a piece of paper and a pen, or a computer and your fingers, and do this for me. **Write down everything in the world that you are thankful for.** All of it. Your mom, your dad, your dog, your bed, the sun, the clouds, your house, your friends, all of it. Make the list as long as you can. Then print it or tear it out of the notebook and put it by your bed. Read it each morning when you wake up and every night when you go to bed. And read it out loud. That helps your brain to really get that life is good and you are so thankful. In fact, you can carry it around with you and read it whenever an idol rears its ugly head. Say a small prayer of thanksgiving and then tell God all the things you are thankful for. It's impossible to be thankful to God and miserable at the same time. Giving thanks will make your heart lighter, your eyes brighter, and your mind clearer. So get to thanking him and watch your idols fade into the background.

EAT ALL YOUR HUMBLE PIE

> Then Jesus said to his disciples, "If anyone would come after me, he must deny himself and take up his cross and follow me."
>
> Matthew 16:24

> Do nothing out of selfish ambition or vain conceit, but in humility consider others better than yourselves. Each of you should look not only to your own interests, but also to the interests of others.
>
> Philippians 2:3–4

The sixth way to stay idol free is to practice humility. This is a lot like the dying to self stuff we already talked about. Jesus talked a lot about taking up the cross, dying to self, and being humble. And they all sound really unsafe and even kind of stupid when you think about it, but the truth is that this kind of lifestyle will set you free from the bondage of idolatry. **Humility is** defined by *Harper's Bible Dictionary* as **"a socially acknowledged claim to**

neutrality in the competition of life." I love that def. It means you don't have to compete for attention, acceptance, or understanding, because when you do, you lose. People are right when they say you can't please all the people all the time, and when you try, you just fail and feel miserable. **Humility is the best form of dying to self because it says, "I'm not the one who is important; God is."** The *Tyndale Bible Dictionary* says it's **"an ungrudging and unhypocritical acknowledgment of absolute dependence upon God."** And that's the exact opposite of idolatry. When you practice humility, you starve out the idols that demand you feed your "needs" and theirs.

Since humility is such a huge concept, I won't be able to cover it all here, but you can check out more about it at www.askhayley. com. Look for the devotional link. For now, **here are a few ways to help you think about and practice humility so that you may be idol free:**

1. Don't think you're better because of the things that happen to you. When you have major victories or you are super successful, don't brag or gloat over how good you are. That is the exact opposite of being humble.

King David understood humility and reliance on God instead of self when he said, "But who am I and who are my people that we should be able to offer as generously as this? For all things come from You, and from Your hand we have given You" (1 Chronicles 29:14 NASB).

2. Don't cut yourself down; just have an honest opinion of yourself. Cutting yourself down might feel like humility, but it's actually the exact opposite. When you cut yourself down, you are really hoping for someone to correct you and tell you how great you are. It's fishing. It's not humility. The humble person knows that they are God's creation and that self-condemnation is a self or inward focus, not a God focus. So look up, not in, in order to be humble.

> These are matters which have, to be sure, the appearance of wisdom in self-made religion and <u>self-abasement and severe treatment of the body, but are of no value against fleshly indulgence.</u>
>
> Colossians 2:23 NASB

3. Be okay when others think of you just as lowly as you do. If you have humility, you can never be cut down or hurt by anyone's comments because you know yourself that you are not perfect. You're as sinful as they assume, if not worse. When you practice humility, you don't resent the tough stuff you go through because you are sure that everything that happens to you is the result of God's wise and loving purpose for you.

> Consider it pure joy, my brothers, whenever you face trials of many kinds, because you know that the testing of your faith develops perseverance. Perseverance must finish its work so that you may be mature and complete, not lacking anything.
>
> James 1:2–4

Humility seems like an archaic concept practiced only by Mother Teresa and the apostle Paul, but the truth is that it is commanded by Christ himself. It is more than applicable to your life; it's a necessity. If you are willing to risk trusting God and you believe his Word to be true—all of it—then you must practice humility. I don't expect you to be an expert in one day; it will take a lifetime of standing up and falling down. You won't ever fully conquer it until you get to heaven, but it needs to be a goal for each of us. And remember, Jesus promises us that those who humble themselves will be lifted up.

> For whoever exalts himself will be humbled, and whoever humbles himself will be exalted.
>
> Matthew 23:12

Who do you think is more powerful, you or God? Of course, we both know the answer. So if God is more powerful, then why wouldn't you trust yourself to him rather than you? You can only lift yourself up so far before you can expect God to humble you. Ouch! Don't want that. But if you let go and humble yourself, you can trust the all-powerful God to lift you up. Sounds like the most sensible option to me.

I could talk about humility all day. It's a huge concept and a really hard one. But I encourage you to explore it some more. Read God's Word; there are some verses in the back of this book if you want to get to it quickly. Study it, pray about it, and work toward true humility. And you will be exalted!

More Ways to Practice Humility

- Do your good works in private (Matthew 6:1).

- Never fish for compliments or praise yourself (Luke 14:7–11).

- When you get applause for doing something, deflect the praise to God (Ephesians 1:3).

- Compliment and praise people (Matthew 7:12).

- Be happy when other people are being applauded, even if you aren't (Matthew 20:1–16).

- Never compare yourself with others unless you are trying to make them look good (Matthew 23:12).

- Don't keep making excuses for yourself (Proverbs 3:7).

- Thank God for all of your weaknesses, faults, and imperfections (James 1:9).

- Be content whatever happens to you (Philippians 4:11).

- If God is testing you through trials or persecution, humble yourself before him to ease your pain (2 Chronicles 32:26).

MEMORIZE GOD

The final thing I'm going to say about being idol free is that **you have to agree with God.** And one of the best ways to agree with him on things is to know what he says. Memorizing Scripture really helps your mind and heart to get it. I like to find those verses that really apply to what I'm dealing with and memorize those so that whenever an idol rears its ugly head, I can beat it down with God's Word. The thing to remember with all the temptations to worship idols is that *"No temptation has seized you except what is common to man. And God is faithful; he will not let you be tempted beyond what you can bear. But when you are tempted, he will also provide a way out so that you can stand up under it"* (1 Corinthians 10:13). So memorize all the Scripture that you can, and never forget that you can be and are commanded to be free from idols.

SUMMING IT UP

Becoming idol free is going to be hard work. But God is right beside you and ready to get to work. It's time to take your idols seriously and get to work avoiding them, shattering them, and giving them over to God. If you are tough enough to read God's Word and learn to live by it, then you are sure to feel the joy of being idol free! Dive in and trust God to be true to his Word. You can do this. Here's a quick rundown of the basics of getting idol free. Check out diagram 3 below.

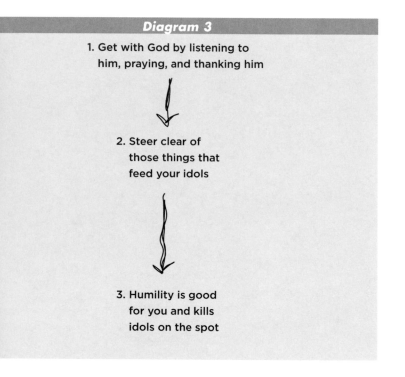

Diagram 3

1. Get with God by listening to him, praying, and thanking him

2. Steer clear of those things that feed your idols

3. Humility is good for you and kills idols on the spot

WORKING IT OUT

Clean house. So if you're really ready to do this, then you're going to have to do some housecleaning. The idols you have loved for so long have dug into your life and made themselves at home. They've moved into not only your heart and mind but your house as well. After you pray and work through things with God, do a walk-through of your living space. What do you see around you that feeds your idols? Romance novels? Credit cards? Your favorite idol smiling at you from a poster on your wall? Look in every nook and cranny, find all those tasty treats that keep your idols fat and happy, and get rid of them, or at least reduce your intake for your light idols. This stuff is only bringing you farther and farther from God, and so it's time to say good-bye. So clean house and remove everything that begs you to take your eyes off of God.

Here's a little list to get you kick-started. Look it over for your idols and see what's feeding them:

Shopping—cut up your credit cards; trash all your catalogs and mags

Music—check your playlists; less Fergie, more Plumb

Your favorite sports team—redo your room to get rid of the team colors; take the posters off the wall; put away your pom-poms

Looking good—get rid of all but the bathroom mirror; throw away all but the basics when it comes to makeup; give some clothes to charity

Your favorite hobby—put it away for a while

Superstition—throw out your lucky rabbit's foot or St. Christopher medal

Astrology—throw out or burn up anything with a sign on it

Addiction—get rid of anything like drugs, alcohol, or posters of such things; lose all the phone numbers of suppliers and friends who use

"Once you decide to be idol free, you're going to notice that you are getting **closer to God.**"

Hayley DiMarco

THE HAPPY ENDING

(or, The Joyous Conclusion)

Well, I know it's been a hard journey. You've done your work well. But the truth is that **breaking your idols not only is obedience to God but also will change your life in a really good way.** Idols control more than most of us know, and the lies they tell can sound familiar and comforting, but the truth is that the worship of anything other than the true living God will lead ultimately to your destruction. But now that you know all that and you've spotted your idols, I want you to know that you have some things to look forward to. The first thing is joy. True joy, real happiness, can only be yours when you get rid of your idols. I've already talked a lot about this, so I hope you now know that because idols steal your happiness, once they're broken, true happy can flow. But there's more: **once you decide to be idol free, you're going to notice that you are getting closer to God.** And that's because you're going to start loving him more. That might not seem possible, but it's true. Your love affair with God will grow.

There was a sinful woman in Bible days; she was probably a prostitute. She found out where Jesus was having dinner. She went to him and cleaned his feet with a bottle of her perfume. In those days people washed their guests' feet when they came over because the roads were all muddy and dusty. The guy who invited Jesus to dinner hadn't even dusted Jesus's feet, and in came this woman who used a beautiful and expensive perfume to clean him. The rest of the guys at the party were all in a tizzy because she was "wasting good perfume" on feet cleaning. Why was she going all overboard? She even started crying and wiping his feet with her hair! Wow, she had it bad for Jesus. It says in Luke 7:44–47, "Then he turned toward the woman and said to Simon, 'Do you see this woman? I came into your house. You did not give me any water for my feet, but she wet my feet with her tears and wiped them with her hair. You did not give me a kiss, but this woman, from the time I entered, has not stopped kissing my feet. You did not put oil on my head, but she has poured perfume on my feet. Therefore, I tell you, her many sins have been forgiven—for she loved much. But he who has been forgiven little loves little.'"

This woman clearly loved Jesus more than the others. Why? According to Jesus, it was because she had a lot of stuff that she had done wrong and he forgave. Many times when you've had a lot of junk that's been forgiven, you end up loving God more because of all he's brought you through. This is why getting rid of your idols will naturally draw you closer to God. What an amazing experience to be close to the one who loves you more than anyone else in the world!

But wait, there's more. Part of what you need in order to break your idols is to read and learn God's Word. The more you need him, the more you will read him. And because of that, one of the results of getting rid of your idols will be that you will know more about the Bible and how it relates to your life. Have you ever wanted to be more like those people who seem to know right where to look in the Bible for help? Those people who can recite the chapter and verse as easy as peazy? Well, that can be you too. The more you fight your idols away with God's Word, the more it will be committed to your memory. So another bonus of getting rid of your idols is knowing your way around God's Word better.

As you get to know God's Word more, you will notice a couple of recurring themes. They are humility and obedience. On the surface they might seem like really weak and annoying traits that in the past you didn't want much to do with. But the truth is that both of these godly character traits lead to peace, hope, and joy. When you are obedient to God's Word, you don't have to stress and worry about your life. He gives you the answers you need and the hope you crave. And when you truly humble yourself and trust him who has forgiven you much with the entirety of your life, your happiness and peace will grow. Yep, ditching your idols is a mighty good way to go.

I know it's going to be hard to do all the stuff in this book, but just know that I am right there with you, as are a bazillion other girls on this planet who seek to know God and to truly fall deeply and passionately in love with him. Those of us who do this know that God is capable of helping us and doesn't hate us when hard times come. He is the king of the universe, ruler of all, and he loves us. But through the trials and the suffering in our lives, he looks into the heart of us all and searches all that we are. He judges the character of each of us during trials and tribulation, during hard times and good. Therefore, as God makes himself seen in the fire, so our true hearts are shown in those deciding moments of our lives when we say no to sin's taunts and hello to God's gentle whisper.

At one time your idols might have seemed like your friends, but now I pray that you can see them for what they really are. Please stand with me in the commitment to break all the idols in your life and to help those around you do the same thing. Now that you've read *Idol Girls*, I challenge you to find a friend and teach them what you've learned. Take the lessons here and ask your friend not only to help you smash your idols but also to join you by smashing their own. This book has a lot of self-analysis stuff that can help you do this huge task, so make sure your friend has her own copy so she can do the same stuff you did. Then get together weekly, chat daily, and hold each other accountable to the idol-smashing you are committed to.

Once you've got a buddy on board, talk to your youth pastor or leader and ask him or her if they would like to do an *Idol Girls* study for your whole group. You'll find info about that in the back of the book. You can even download discussion guides for studying in a group at www.hungryplanet.net along with study guides for my other books. Don't let the words you've read here fall on deaf ears. It's time to take action, but don't do it alone—bring other idol girls with you and prove to the enemy that he is losing power, one girl at a time!

Well, my sister, it's been a wonderful ride. Thanks for taking it with me. Pray for me and I'll pray for you. Stay strong and stay in touch. Remember, if you have any tough questions, send them over to www.askhayley.com. You can win this battle; I know you can. And so does God. This book came to you for a reason. Don't let that very important reason pass without taking the steps you know you need to take!

Bye for now—love,
Hayley

Pass It On

If you want to do more work on the subject of idols, check out the *Idol Girls Bible Study* (coming soon!) or go online to www.hungryplanet.net and find a free downloadable curriculum for a group of girls to go through together.

"But the fruit of the Spirit is love, joy, peace, patience, kindness, goodness, faithfulness, gentleness, and self-control."

Galatians 5:22–23

GOD'S WORD, YOUR POWER

CONFESSION

Therefore confess your sins to each other and pray for each other so that you may be healed. The prayer of a righteous man is powerful and effective.

James 5:16

If we confess our sins, he is faithful and just and will forgive us our sins and purify us from all unrighteousness.

1 John 1:9

For it is with your heart that you believe and are justified, and it is with your mouth that you confess and are saved.

Romans 10:10

HAPPINESS

You have filled my heart with greater joy than when their grain and new wine abound.

Psalm 4:7

But the fruit of the Spirit is love, joy, peace, patience, kindness, goodness, faithfulness, gentleness, and self-control.

Galatians 5:22–23

Then they worshiped him and returned to Jerusalem with great joy.

Luke 24:52

My spirit rejoices in God my Savior.

Luke 1:47

I am coming to you now, but I say these things while I am still in the world, so that they may have the full measure of my joy within them.

John 17:13

Rejoice in that day and leap for joy, because great is your reward in heaven.

Luke 6:23

HOPE

As it is written: "No eye has seen, no ear has heard, no mind has conceived what God has prepared for those who love him."

1 Corinthians 2:9

I pray also that the eyes of your heart may be enlightened in order that you may know the hope to which he has called you, the riches of his glorious inheritance in the saints.

Ephesians 1:18

Now we know that if the earthly tent we live in is destroyed, we have a building from God, an eternal house in heaven, not built by human hands. Meanwhile we groan, longing to be clothed with our heavenly dwelling.

2 Corinthians 5:1–2

Yet this I call to mind and therefore I have hope: Because of the LORD's great love we are not consumed, for his compassions never fail. They are new every morning; great is your faithfulness. I say to myself, "The LORD is my portion; therefore I will wait for him." The LORD is good to those whose hope is in him, to the one who seeks him.

Lamentations 3:21–25

HUMILITY

Take my yoke upon you and learn from me, for I am gentle and humble in heart, and you will find rest for your souls.

Matthew 11:29

Therefore, whoever humbles himself like this child is the greatest in the kingdom of heaven.

Matthew 18:4

For whoever exalts himself will be humbled, and whoever humbles himself will be exalted.

Matthew 23:12

For he has been mindful of the humble state of his servant. From now on all generations will call me blessed.

Luke 1:48

He has brought down rulers from their thrones but has lifted up the humble.

Luke 1:52

I tell you that this man [who knew he was a sinner], rather than the other, went home justified before God. For everyone who exalts himself will be humbled, and he who humbles himself will be exalted.

Luke 18:14

"Has not my hand made all these things, and so they came into being?" declares the LORD. "This is the one I esteem: he who is humble and contrite in spirit, and trembles at my word."

Isaiah 66:2

A man's pride brings him low, but a man of lowly spirit gains honor.

Proverbs 29:23

Better to be lowly in spirit and among the oppressed than to share plunder with the proud.

Proverbs 16:19

IDOLS

Love the Lord your God with all your heart and with all your soul
and with all your mind and with all your strength.

Mark 12:30

No temptation has seized you except what is common to man.
And God is faithful; he will not let you be tempted beyond what
you can bear. But when you are tempted, he will also provide a
way out so that you can stand up under it. Therefore, my dear
friends, flee from idolatry.

1 Corinthians 10:13–14

And the LORD struck the people with a plague because of what
they did with the calf Aaron had made.

Exodus 32:35

Do not love the world or anything in the world. If anyone loves
the world, the love of the Father is not in him. For everything in
the world—the cravings of sinful man, the lust of his eyes and the
boasting of what he has and does—comes not from the Father but
from the world. The world and its desires pass away, but the man
who does the will of God lives forever.

1 John 2:15–17

I will stretch out my hand against Judah and against all who live in
Jerusalem. I will cut off from this place every remnant of Baal, the
names of the pagan and the idolatrous priests—those who bow
down on the roofs to worship the starry host, those who bow down
and swear by the LORD and who also swear by Molech.

Zephaniah 1:4–5

As Solomon grew old, his wives turned his heart after other gods, and his heart was not fully devoted to the LORD his God, as the heart of David his father had been.

1 Kings 11:4

Do not follow other gods to serve and worship them; do not provoke me to anger with what your hands have made. Then I will not harm you.

Jeremiah 25:6

They rejected his decrees and the covenant he had made with their fathers and the warnings he had given them. They followed worthless idols and themselves became worthless. They imitated the nations around them although the LORD had ordered them, "Do not do as they do," and they did the things the LORD had forbidden them to do They forsook all the commands of the LORD their God and made for themselves two idols cast in the shape of calves, and an Asherah pole. They bowed down to all the starry hosts, and they worshiped Baal. They sacrificed their sons and daughters in the fire. They practiced divination and sorcery and sold themselves to do evil in the eyes of the LORD, provoking him to anger. So the LORD was very angry with Israel and removed them from his presence. Only the tribe of Judah was left.

2 Kings 17:15–18

All who make idols are nothing, and the things they treasure are worthless. Those who would speak up for them are blind; they are ignorant, to their own shame.

Isaiah 44:9

THE NEW YOU

He himself bore our sins in his body on the tree, so that we might die to sins and live for righteousness; by his wounds you have been healed.

1 Peter 2:24

[Christ] gave himself for us to redeem us from all wickedness and to purify for himself a people that are his very own, eager to do what is good.

Titus 2:14

For you died, and your life is now hidden with Christ in God.

Colossians 3:3

Surely you heard of him and were taught in him in accordance with the truth that is in Jesus. You were taught, with regard to your former way of life, to put off your old self, which is being corrupted by its deceitful desires; to be made new in the attitude of your minds; and to put on the new self, created to be like God in true righteousness and holiness.

Ephesians 4:21–24

But if Christ is in you, your body is dead because of sin, yet your spirit is alive because of righteousness.

Romans 8:10

PRAYER

Let us then approach the throne of grace with confidence, so that we may receive mercy and find grace to help us in our time of need.

Hebrews 4:16

Again, I tell you that if two of you on earth agree about anything you ask for, it will be done for you by my Father in heaven.

Matthew 18:19

On reaching the place, he said to them, "Pray that you will not fall into temptation."

Luke 22:40

This is the confidence we have in approaching God: that if we ask anything according to his will, he hears us. And if we know that he hears us —whatever we ask—we know that we have what we asked of him.

1 John 5:14–15

SUFFERING

To this you were called, because Christ suffered for you, leaving you an example, that you should follow in his steps.

1 Peter 2:21

For it has been granted to you on behalf of Christ not only to believe on him, but also to suffer for him.

Philippians 1:29

For our light and momentary troubles are achieving for us an eternal glory that far outweighs them all.

2 Corinthians 4:17

Therefore, since Christ suffered in his body, arm yourselves also with the same attitude, because he who has suffered in his body is done with sin.

1 Peter 4:1

Although he was a son, he learned obedience from what he suffered.

Hebrews 5:8

Dear friends, do not be surprised at the painful trial you are suffering, as though something strange were happening to you. But rejoice that you participate in the sufferings of Christ, so that you may be overjoyed when his glory is revealed.

1 Peter 4:12–13

Hayley DiMarco writes cutting-edge and bestselling books including *Mean Girls: Facing Your Beauty Turned Beast, Marriable: Taking the Desperate Out of Dating, Dateable: Are You? Are They?, The Dateable Rules,* and *The Dirt on Breaking Up.* Her goal is to give practical answers for life's problems and encourage girls to form stronger spiritual lives. From traveling the world with a French theater troupe to working for a little shoe company called Nike, Hayley has seen a lot of life and decided to make a difference in her world. Hayley is Chief Creative Officer and founder of Hungry Planet, an independent publishing imprint and communications company that feeds the world's appetite for truth. Hungry Planet helps organizations understand and reach the multitasking mind-set, while Hungry Planet books tackle life's everyday issues with a distinctly modern spiritual voice.

To keep the conversation going log on to
www.nomoreidols.com.

And for more on Hayley's other books
check out
www.hungryplanet.net

"Feeding the World's Appetite for Truth"

What makes Hungry Planet books different?

Every Hungry Planet book attacks the senses of the reader with a postmodern mind-set (both visually and mentally) in a way unlike most books in the marketplace. Attention to every detail from physical appearance (book size, titling, cover, and interior design) to message (content and author's voice) helps Hungry Planet books connect with the more "visual" reader in ways that ordinary books can't.

   With writing and packaging content for the young adult and "hip adult" markets, Hungry Planet books combine cutting-edge design with felt-need topics, all the while injecting a much-needed spiritual voice.

Why are publishers so eager to work with Hungry Planet?

Because of the innovative success and profitable track record of HP projects from the bestselling *Dateable* and *Mean Girls* to the Gold Medallion–nominated *The Dirt on Sex* (part of HP's The Dirt series). Publishers also take notice of HP founder Hayley DiMarco's past success in creating big ideas like the "Biblezine" concept while she was brand manager for Thomas Nelson Publishers' teen book division.

How does Hungry Planet come up with such big ideas?

Hayley and HP general manager/husband Michael DiMarco tend to create their best ideas at mealtime, which in the DiMarco household is around five times a day. Once the big idea and scope of the topic are established, the couple decides either to write the content themselves or find an up-and-coming author with a passion for the topic. HP then partners with a publisher to create the book.

How do I find out more about Hungry Planet?

Use the Web, silly—www.hungryplanet.net

COULD it all Be just a Big misUNDERstaNDiNg?

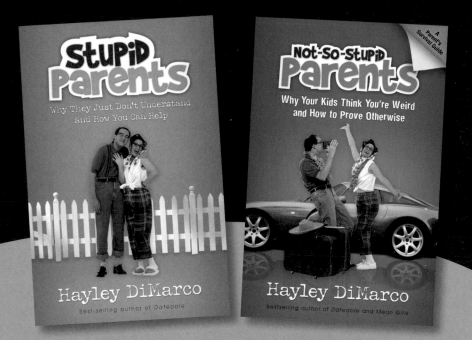

StUPiD PARents
Why They Just Don't Understand and How You Can Help
Hayley DiMarco
Best-selling author of Dateable

Not-So-StUPiD Parents
A Parent's Survival Guide
Why Your Kids Think You're Weird and How to Prove Otherwise
Hayley DiMarco
Bestselling author of Dateable and Mean Girls

Let's face it. You feel like your Parents just DoN't UNDERstaND.
And you probably don't understand them either! All you want is some space, freedom, and respect. It can be hard when you feel like you're from totally different planets. But fear not! There's hope. With a book for you and a book for them, find out how to stop arguing, start talking, and finally understand each other so everyone can get along before you leave the nest.

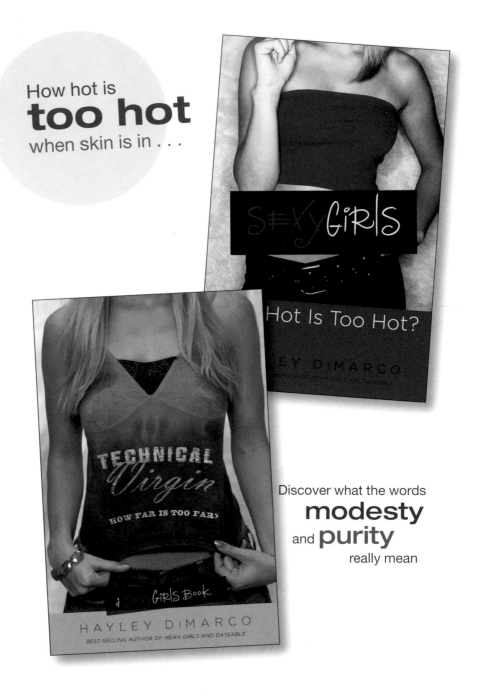

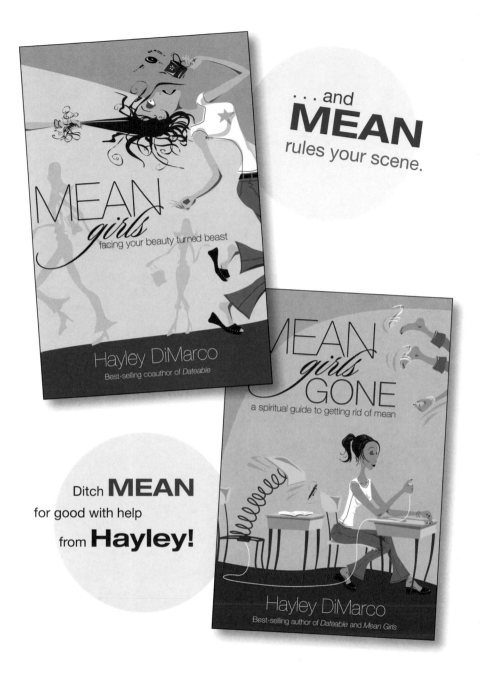

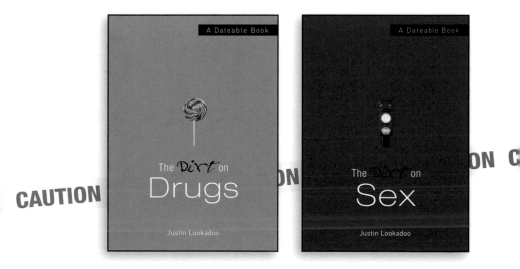

Got Questions?

Get answers.